"So, this is that awkward moment at the end of our date where I want to kiss you again but I don't want to overstep any boundaries. Since we're still getting to know each other, it might be too soon. And I would hate to get slapped."

Naomi giggled, her eyes shifting in a slight roll. "Do you often get slapped when you kiss a woman?"

He grinned. "Not at all. But if I kiss you, it won't be like last time. It won't be a casual kiss on the cheek. Or a light peck on your lips. This time I plan to kiss you like you've never been kissed before."

"Well, if I'm honest with you," Naomi started, her weight shifting from side to side, "this is that moment where I want to be kissed but I don't want you to think that I'm too forward. I wouldn't want you to get the wrong impression of me. Because I am *not* that kind of woman."

Patrick leaned to drop his bag onto the coffee table. He took a step toward her, closing the distance between them.

Dear Reader,

Let me warn you by saying there is nothing *sweet* about *Sweet Stallion*! Ms. Naomi Stallion is not the sugary sibling. As the eldest girl of the Utah Stallions, she is not known to hold her tongue and you'll discover that she has no problems laying it all on the table.

Legal eagle Patrick O'Brien is a delectable mélange of yummy goodness! His attraction to Naomi is instant and the two light up the pages! I think you're going to love, love, love everything about them.

I really like this story! Naomi gives me all kinds of feel-good moments and Patrick just takes my breath away!

As always, thank you so much for your continued support. I am humbled by all the love you keep showing me, my characters and our stories. I know that none of this would be possible without you.

Until the next time, please take care and may God's blessings be with you always.

With much love,

Deborah Fletcher Mello

www.DeborahMello.Blogspot.com

SWEET
Stallion

DEBORAH FLETCHER MELLO

HARLEQUIN® KIMANI™ ROMANCE

Recycling programs
for this product may
not exist in your area.

ISBN-13: 978-0-373-86513-0

Sweet Stallion

Copyright © 2017 by Deborah Fletcher Mello

For questions and comments about the quality of this book please contact us
at CustomerService@Harlequin.com.

HHARLEQUIN®
™ www.Harlequin.com

Printed in U.S.A.

Having been writing since forever, **Deborah Fletcher Mello** can't imagine herself doing anything else. Her first novel, *Take Me to Heart*, earned her a 2004 Romance Slam Jam nomination for Best New Author. In 2008, Deborah won an RT Reviewers' Choice award for Best Series Romance for *Tame a Wild Stallion*. Deborah received a BRAB 2015 Reading Warrior Award for Best Series for her Stallion family series. Deborah was also named the 2016 Romance Slam Jam Author of the Year. In addition, she has received accolades from several publications, including *Publishers Weekly*, *Library Journal*, and *RT Book Reviews*. With each new book, Deborah continues to create unique story lines and memorable characters. Born and raised in Connecticut, Deborah now considers home to be wherever the moment moves her.

Books by Deborah Fletcher Mello

Harlequin Kimani Romance

Passionate Premiere
Truly Yours
Hearts Afire
Twelve Days of Pleasure
My Stallion Heart
Stallion Magic
Tuscan Heat
A Stallion's Touch
A Pleasing Temptation
Sweet Stallion

Visit the Author Profile page
at Harlequin.com for more titles.

To my Diamonds,

Thank you for your support and encouragement.

You give selflessly each and every day,
and I am grateful for you!

Chapter 1

Naomi Stallion was standing in her big brother's kitchen when he and his wife came through the front door of their Arlington Drive home. The couple was giggling, their voices low. Naomi winced, suspecting that she was about to intrude on an intimate moment. She called out to them, rattling a frying pan against the stove top as she did.

"Hello! It's me! I'm here in your kitchen. Please don't take your clothes off!" she shouted, remembering the last time the two had come running through the house not knowing she was there.

There was a brief moment of silence, and then laughter led Noah Stallion and Catherine "Cat" Moore-Stallion from their living room into the dining area.

"Hi, Naomi!" Cat chimed as she toyed with the buttons on her blouse and adjusted her skirt.

Naomi smiled. "Sorry about that."

"Hey!" Noah said. He tossed up a casual hand as his eyes widened curiously. "What are you doing here?"

Naomi gave her brother a look. Before she could respond, Cat interrupted, exclaiming excitedly, "You cooked!"

"I did. I figured it was the least I could do after showing up unannounced," Naomi responded. "To stay for a few days," she added, the words coming rapidly. "Maybe even a week. Or two."

The couple laughed, the two exchanging a look between them.

"So, to what do we owe the honor?" Noah asked as he moved toward the counter and settled down on a wooden stool. He reached for a stalk of celery that rested on a vegetable tray Naomi had pushed in his direction. "We weren't expecting to see you until next month."

"I wasn't expecting to be here. But what about you? I'm actually surprised that you two aren't in New York. Isn't that where one of you was supposed to be?"

Noah nodded. "My plans changed. I needed to be at the corporate office here, and Cat flew in to see me before she heads to Dallas tomorrow."

Naomi gave them both a smile. "My plans changed, too. The property adjacent to my farm is going up for auction next week. I want that land. If I can get it, I want to expand my business model here and get a second food co-op up and running."

The farm Naomi referred to was the fifteen acres of land she owned in the Pleasant Grove area just outside downtown Salt Lake City. It had been a foreclosure investment that she'd acquired years ago, initially planning to wait for the real estate market to improve, and then sell it. Her decision to actually grow produce on the property and work it had come as a surprise to them all.

"How much land is it?" Cat asked, joining her husband at the counter. She reached for her own celery stick and dipped it into the cucumber dressing that filled a small bowl.

"It's a good fifty acres. There's an open house tomorrow and I plan to go walk it in the morning and talk to the Realtor handling the sale."

Noah cut a quick glance at his wife, who was licking the dressing from her fingers. Naomi noted his expression, the color heating his cheeks as he bit down on his bottom lip. Cat laughed and Naomi rolled her eyes.

"I guess I should have called first," Naomi said, a wry smile pulling across her face. "But I'm so used to just letting myself in I didn't think about it. Now that you're married, I should probably give your key back, big brother."

Noah shook his head. "You're here more than we are."

"And you are always welcome here," Cat added. "Don't you even think about giving him that key back. This is your home, too."

Naomi rounded the marble counter to give her sister-in-law a hug. "I really appreciate that." She winked at her brother. "I still like this one. I'm glad you're keeping her."

Noah laughed. "So, what did you cook? Since I can't get any *dessert* just yet, I might as well enjoy some dinner."

"Noah! Really?" Cat laughed. "I can't believe you just said that!"

He shrugged, his bright smile filling his face. "It's the truth!"

Naomi shook her head. "Set the table and we can eat. I cooked your favorite—vegetable lasagna."

"That's not my favorite. I was hoping for something battered and fried with lots of cheese and gravy. Not vegetable lasagna. And I bet you put tofu in it, too."

"Tofu is good for you."

"I hate tofu."

"No, you don't."

"Yes, I do!"

"Really, you don't," Naomi said, eyeing him with a raised brow.

Cat laughed. "Well, I didn't have to cook it so I love whatever it is."

"She doesn't cook for me. Do you still think I should keep her?" Noah asked teasingly.

"I do great takeout and I'm a master at other things you like," Cat responded as she leaned against her husband, pressing a kiss to his cheek.

"I will have me some dessert tonight," he muttered against her ear.

"I made yogurt parfaits with fresh fruit," Naomi interjected, grinning at the two of them.

"I'll enjoy that, too," her brother said smugly.

Naomi waved a dismissive hand in Noah's direction as she returned to the oven.

Minutes later the trio sat at the dining table, laughing heartily as they caught up on the family news. Naomi was the second oldest sibling and the eldest girl in their close-knit family. The twins, Nicholas and Nathaniel, were only a year behind her in age and their sister Natalie was the baby in the family. It had been a few years since she and her siblings had lost their mother, Norris Jean Stallion, after a brief illness. But other than his name, they knew very little about their father. Noah had always acted as their surrogate parent, supporting them when they needed it most.

Watching Noah as he and his wife flirted shamelessly with each other made Naomi smile. Her brother was happier than she could ever remember him. He and Cat had been each other's grade school crush and had reconnected at their high school reunion. They'd been inseparable ever since. Of all her siblings, Naomi was closest to Noah, both overly protective of the others, and he was one of her best friends. She trusted him with everything.

Her brother had been her biggest cheerleader when she'd purchased her first property, intending to make it the organic mecca of Utah. Despite her best efforts, the timing hadn't worked for her. Then their mother's health had started to decline and the older woman's demanding nature had made it nearly impossible for Naomi to do all that she needed to do for herself. Shortly after, a beloved friend had afforded her the opportunity of a lifetime, bequeathing her an established farm in Phoenix, Arizona. Making the decision to leave Salt Lake City had been one of the hardest she'd ever had to make, but Noah had insisted, gently shoving her in the direction of her future.

Within a few short months of her getting settled and comfortable, the farm and her organic foods business, Vitally Vegan, had taken off and thrived. It had become everything Naomi had imagined and more. Now, she saw the opportunity to expand her business to her hometown as a large blessing in disguise.

Cat interrupted her thoughts. "This was good, Naomi. Thank you," she said, as she swiped a paper napkin across her mouth.

"It was really good!" Noah echoed, sliding his index finger around his parfait cup to lick away the last of the strawberry and yogurt.

"Thank you. I'm glad you both enjoyed it."

"Are you cooking tomorrow, too?" Noah asked, his tone teasing.

Naomi grinned. "Are you going to be here?"

Her brother nodded. "I am, and if you want me to, I can go with you in the morning before I head into the office. It's been a while since I was last at your farm and I'd like to see the land you're interested in."

"I'd really like that. I could use a second opinion."

Noah laughed. "I know you wanted to ask."

Naomi grinned. "I did, but I didn't want to interrupt anything else you might have going on."

"Oh, you're not interrupting anything," he said as he rose from his seat. He leaned over, kissing the top of her head. "Not a thing," he added as he winked at her. He reached for his wife's hand. "We will see you in the morning."

Catherine giggled as she allowed her husband to pull her to her feet and down the hall toward the master bedroom. She called out over her shoulder, "Good night, Naomi!"

Naomi laughed heartily. "Good night!" she said, and then she heard the bedroom door close and lock behind them.

With the dishes washed and put away and the kitchen returned to its usual immaculate condition, Naomi retired to the spare bedroom at the other end of the ranch-style home. Thinking about her brother and his wife made her smile. It also made her a bit misty-eyed. Would there ever be a day when she might know a love like theirs? It was only when she was in Utah, visiting with the duo, or talking to her sister, Natalie, and her husband, Tinjin, who lived in Paris, that she even thought about romance and love and a man who could be more than a friend in her life. Any other time she was too busy to give that kind of nonsense any consideration. She blew a soft sigh past her lips as she changed into her nightclothes, donning an old T-shirt and a pair of track shorts. She twisted the length of her hair into a high pineapple atop her head and wrapped the thick tresses with a silk scarf.

Naomi pushed the thoughts away, and the emotion they brought, as she crawled into bed with a file folder of documents about the property that had her interest. She reviewed the plat, making note of the property lines, and then examined the tax records. It would be a challenge, but if she could expand her crop, she would turn a quick profit in no time. She jotted her ideas down on a lined composition pad, doodling where she imagined Swiss chard and an assortment of beans being planted.

The existing farm already sourced sweet Spanish onions, celery, tomatoes and peppers to local restaurants. Along with the added land and produce, she would be able to promote a sustainable food system to consumers through a co-op, making natural, organic produce more affordable to the community. Just envisioning how she hoped to see her dream grow excited her. Figuring out the work that it would take wiped all thoughts of not having a man from her mind.

An hour later Naomi gathered the papers together and returned them neatly to the manila folder. After setting them on the nightstand beside the bed, she checked her cell phone one last time for any missed messages. Finding none, she plugged it into the charger, then dropped to her knees on the carpeted floor.

Her prayers were swift as she whispered the childhood chant their mother had made them recite nightly, and her own appeals for mercy, strength and guidance. With the litany billowing skyward, she crawled back into the queen-size bed and pulled the covers up around her lean frame. Minutes later, she was sound asleep.

Chapter 2

The morning sun was shining brightly, indicative of the high temperatures that had been forecast. The sky was mostly clear, a rich shade of blue dotted with an occasional cloud. Everything about the landscape fulfilled Naomi's wish list, and it took all her fortitude not to jump up and down like an excited five-year-old. The property itself was slightly overgrown, with high grasses interspersed with patches of brown dirt. There was a small abandoned home, condemned by the city, two outbuildings, a tree here and there, and nothing else but open air as far as the eye could see.

This was the only morning that the property was accessible for viewing, and several real estate agents in hiking boots or running shoes were tramping through with perspective buyers. Naomi eyed them all, trying to be as inconspicuous as possible as she tried to assess who might be her most serious competition. She ruled out the two women who'd shown up in high heels and designer dresses, both fanning away imaginary bugs from their newly coiffed hairdos. Eavesdropping on their conversation made it clear that neither had any interest in the property; they'd stopped only because they'd seen the open-house signs along the road. It seemed to be the case for many, who took one look at the abandoned house—an amalgamation of rotted wood, rust and mold—and scurried back to their vehicles, anxious to be far from the land Naomi coveted. There were a few men who seemed to be there with purpose, but only one or two looked like they might be interested in giving her a run for her money.

Naomi and Noah stood beneath a tent that had been pitched as a makeshift information center for perspective buyers. A Realtor from Cushman and Wakefield was pulling papers from a file folder that rested on a folding table. Other agents were trying to stir up interest from the few people standing with them, to no avail. The chatter shifted from hushed whispers to lighthearted quips and back. There were only a few serious questions posed, and most had come from Naomi.

Noah took a step closer to her, leaning in to speak without being overheard. "Someone's got their eye on you!" he said, his singsong tone reminding her of when they'd been much younger and he would tease her about some boy having a crush on her.

Naomi's eyes darted back and forth. "Who? What?" she whispered back.

Noah laughed. "Behind you. In the corner. Working his Rico Suave looks. Don't turn around!" he muttered, grabbing her forearm.

They both froze for a second. "Okay, look now," he told her in a low voice.

She shook her head. "You play too much," she snapped as she tossed a quick look over her shoulder.

The man was standing with his back only slightly to them, but she could see his gaze reaching out into the distance toward where the property bordered hers. He appeared to be lost in thought, oblivious to all else around him. Naomi gasped, so loud that even her brother noticed.

Noah laughed. "Yep! Thought you'd like that!"

"Shut up, Noah," Naomi said, her voice an even lower whisper. She took a deep breath, holding the air at the bottom of her lungs. She shifted her gaze back in the man's direction.

Whoever he was, he was breathtaking. He could have easily graced the cover of any men's magazine. His complexion was butterscotch with an abundance of rich cream. He sported a neatly trimmed mustache and goatee. His auburn hair had deep red undertones and he wore it closely cropped to tame his loose curls. He was dressed in torn jeans, a black cotton T-shirt and paint-stained work boots. On first impression, he looked like one of the many migrant farm workers who made the area their home seasonally, when it came time to pick crops. At the same time, he appeared out of place and slightly uncomfortable.

Naomi was eyeing him intently when he suddenly

turned and they locked gazes. His eyes widened, a hint of surprise teasing the edges of his dark orbs. They stared and then his full lips lifted in a bright smile that filled his face.

It wasn't until Noah gave her a light pinch that she felt her own face lift in response, smiling back. She turned abruptly, spinning toward her brother. Her knees were shaking, and for the first time in a very long while, Naomi felt out of control and couldn't explain why.

Patrick O'Brien was still smiling as he moved toward the man and woman standing near the outer edge of the tent. He'd taken notice of the two earlier, when they'd walked from the property across the way. It was the woman who had caught his attention, her lithe frame moving purposely, her arms swinging, her stride closer to a stomp if it hadn't been for the sway of her hips and extremely delectable backside. She had the tiniest waistline of any woman he'd ever seen, and legs that were miles long. Her figure was complimented by formfitting denim jeans, a white button-down blouse and black leather cowboy boots.

He cleared his throat as he reached where they stood, extending his hand toward the man in introduction. "Excuse me, I don't mean to interrupt, but you look very familiar. Have we met before?"

Noah nodded. "Actually, I was just thinking the same thing. At the courthouse, maybe? Probably in passing."

Patrick pondered the comment for a moment before he responded. "You're with the Salt Lake City police department?"

"I was. I'm in private security now. Noah Stallion."

He smiled. "My name's Patrick. Patrick O'Brien. I couldn't help overhearing the conversation you and your wife were having. I was hoping I could ask you a question?"

Naomi's brow rose curiously as she lifted her eyes to stare at the man. Her brother answered for them both.

"Patrick, this is actually my *sister*, Naomi Stallion. She is *not* my wife," he said with a soft chuckle.

Naomi cut her eyes at her brother, grimacing slightly. She shifted her gaze back to the stranger, her palm sliding against his as he shook her hand. The touch was like silk gliding across her flesh, and she mused that he had probably never done a day's worth of hard labor in his life. "It's nice to meet you, Patrick," she answered. "How can we help you?"

"I heard you mention the property next door. Do you mind sharing what you know about it?"

She looked him up and down, her mind's eye assembling a photographic journal for her to muse over later. His eyes were hazel, the rich shade flecked with hints of gold and green. He was tall and solid, his broad chest and thick arms pulling the fabric of his shirt taut. His jeans fit comfortably against a very high and round behind, and he had big feet. Very big feet in expensive, steel-toed work boots. He exuded sex appeal like a beacon. She hadn't missed the looks he was getting from the few women around them, one of whom was openly staring at him as they stood there chatting.

"What would you like to know about Norris Farms?" Naomi asked. She crossed her arms over her chest.

Patrick's smile widened, his cheeks flushing with color. He struggled not to stare, drawing attention to the curve of her cleavage. "Norris," he repeated. "That's an interesting name. Is it a fully functioning farm?"

"It is. They use ecologically-based production systems to produce their foods and fibers. They are certified organic."

"Is there a homestead?"

"There is."

"Have the owners had it long? Is there any family history attached to it?"

Naomi hesitated for a brief second. "May I ask why you're so interested? Are you thinking about bidding on *this* property?"

Patrick clasped his hands behind his back and widened his stance a bit. "I'm actually an attorney. I represent the Perry Group and they're interested in acquiring this lot."

Both Naomi and Noah bristled slightly, exchanging a quick look.

Naomi scoffed, apparent attitude evident in her voice. "The Perry Group?"

Patrick nodded. "Yes. They're a locally owned investment company. Very well established and they—"

Her eyes narrowed as she snapped, "We know who they are."

Patrick looked from one sibling to the other, feeling the rising tension that wafted between them. Frowning in confusion, he dipped his head in a slight nod. "Well, I head their legal department and our planning and development group thinks this would be a great location for their next strip mall project."

"Were you behind the recent efforts to rezone this area?" Naomi asked, remembering the land assessment that could have potentially put her out of business.

"We weren't behind it, but we supported it. Bringing more commercial business to this area would greatly benefit the entire community." He took a slight step toward her, closing the space between them. The rise of her perfume teased his nostrils, the sweet scents of vanilla and patchouli wafting through the air. A wave of heat rose from deep in his midsection, erupting through every nerve ending in his body.

"Not really," Naomi retorted as she took a step back, widening the divide again as she took a deep inhalation of air. She exhaled it slowly past her glossed lips.

Patrick gave her an easy smile. "So, I take it you didn't agree?"

"Not at all. In fact, I opposed it vehemently." She skated her gaze across his face, noting the intensity of his stare. It was heated and unnerving, and she was suddenly anxious to be free from it.

"I'd be curious to know why," he said, seeming intent on drawing her into a lengthy conversation.

Naomi hesitated, then shrugged. "If I had the time, I'd tell you, but that's a long conversation and my brother and I need to get back to work."

"What do you do?" he asked curiously.

Naomi shot him a look, pausing for a second time before she answered, "I own that farm next door."

Patrick's expression lifted in fascination. "So, you

definitely have a concerned interest in who acquires this land."

"I do, and I definitely don't want to see it go to the Perry Group." There was the faintest hint of bitterness in her tone.

He nodded but didn't respond, watching how her long dreadlocks waved effortlessly with every movement of her head. Her hair was thick and abundant, falling to her midback, and he found himself resisting the sudden temptation to twist his fingers in the lengthy strands. He clenched a tight fist against his pant leg.

Noah's expression was smug as his gaze shifted back and forth between them. He extended his hand a second time. "It was nice meeting you, Patrick. And good luck. You're going to need it," he said matter-of-factly.

Patrick chuckled, his head shifting in amusement. "It was a pleasure meeting you, too, Noah," he answered. He looked back at Naomi, his smile widening. "I hope to see you again, Naomi. Maybe at the auction?"

She glanced at him one last time, noting the eagerness in his stare and how the bend of his mouth pinched dimples in his cheeks. There was something about the way he was looking at her that intrigued her, but Naomi pushed the rising sensation away. She took a deep breath and held it, counting silently in her head before blowing it softly out again.

With a slight nod she turned toward the real estate agent who'd been standing in wait with a handful of pamphlets and papers. As the two walked off, Noah hesitated, then tossed Patrick a wide grin, shrugging his broad shoulders. "She'll be there," he said with a light chuckle. "She will definitely be there."

Naomi didn't find her brother's teasing as humorous as he did. He'd been giving her a hard time since they'd finished walking the property. Usually the too-serious sibling, Noah was suddenly the life of the party, his quips and banter more like something she or Natalie would share. She cut her eyes at him, the look expressing her annoyance. But this action only made him laugh harder.

"It really isn't funny," Naomi said, her tone snarky.

Noah laughed. "No, it's actually hilarious. That man had you speechless!"

She rolled her eyes. "He did not."

"He had you something."

"He had me irritated. How could anyone want to work for the Perry Group? He said it like it was something to be proud of."

"He can be proud if he wants," Noah said, his goofy smile turning into a deep frown. "They're a good company. People who work there can't help the kind of man their employer is."

Naomi sighed, her eyes rolling one last time. "Whatever."

"So, what are you going to do if they outbid you? Have you thought about that?"

"The Perry Group is not going to beat me. There is no way I'm going to let that happen."

"I imagine they have access to resources you don't have, Naomi. You might not have a choice."

She scoffed, waving a dismissive hand in her brother's direction, and otherwise didn't bother to respond.

Noah continued, his tone softer, consoling. "Be smart about this, please. Don't let your emotions get in the way of making a wise business decision."

Naomi met the look Noah was giving her with one of her own, both understanding that nothing else needed to be said.

By the time Naomi was ready to settle down for the night, there wasn't much that she didn't know about the Perry Group. It was a large conglomerate of mixed-use shopping centers and mall ventures. If they were successful, outbidding her at auction, the land they were both interested in would become just another residential and business project added to their portfolio.

The company had been founded by Nolan Perry and was currently under the leadership of his son, Garrison. Both were renowned not only for their business acumen, but also for their philanthropic efforts in the community. On paper Nolan Perry was a pillar of the community, beloved by the church he had pastored for many years, and a loving husband and father. His son was following in his footsteps.

Off paper, only a few knew the truth about the man many still called Pastor. But Naomi was aware and so were her siblings. They knew his darkest secrets. They knew, because they *were* his darkest secrets. The five of them. Noah, Natalie, Nicholas, Nathaniel and she were Nolan Perry's biological children. The kids he had never wanted to know. The children he had never bothered to love or provide for.

Naomi stared at the image of her father and his family that looked back at her from her computer screen. Pastor Nolan Perry sat with his beloved wife by his side. Their three children, a son and two daughters, smiled obediently behind them. The Perry children had all benefited from private schooling and a privileged upbringing. Growing up, they had never crossed paths with any of the Stallion siblings, who had lived and gone to school on the other side of the economic tracks. If she were honest with herself, Naomi was glad for it. She would give almost anything to keep it that way, having no interest in a relationship with that side of her family.

She sighed loudly as she finally shut down the laptop, sliding it to the nightstand beside the bed. Naomi had vague memories of her father and his visits to see their mother. The two had been lovers for many years, but she and Noah had been too young to understand why he came and went so sporadically. There had been a time or two when he'd come with candy and sweets for them, but very little else. As a family, they had struggled, more often going without than not. Hunger had been common, new clothes nonexistent and toys a luxury their mother could never afford, raising five children as a single parent.

Growing up, all they'd known about their family was that their mother, Norris Jean, had come from humble beginnings. She had been a teenager herself, pregnant with Noah, when she'd followed their father, a traveling minister, to Utah from Dallas, trusting the promises he'd made to her. Those promises had been broken when Norris Jean discovered the man of her dreams had a wife and another family who were more important to him.

After Noah and Naomi were born, a second string of promises, which had never been fulfilled, led to the birth of the twins, Nicholas and Nathaniel. Their mother should have known better by then. But it wasn't until Natalie had come into the world that Norris Jean finally accepted that the man she loved with all her heart had never loved her enough.

Naomi had never understood their mother's fascination with the man, but Norris Jean Stallion had loved Nolan Perry with every fiber of her being. Sometimes, Naomi thought, she had loved him even more than she had loved her own children. She had loved the tears he made her cry, the pain that had pierced her spirit, the heartbreak that had been the foundation of their illicit relationship. Norris Jean had often prayed for him, begging God to bring him back to her, feeling abandoned when those prayers hadn't been answered. For years, her longing for Nolan Perry had bordered on obsessive.

Naomi imagined that her mother would have always been satisfied if Nolan had kept coming back to her. If he had allowed her to remain hopeful about the two of them having a future together. But then, just like that, he stopped coming, discarding her and her babies as if they had never been anything to him at all. After that Norris Jean became bitter, anger fueling frustration, disappointment tainting her spirit. The woman's heart hardened and what little joy she'd known had evaporated like mist under a summer sun.

Naomi and Noah had been old enough to remember the storm when it had come crashing down upon them. They remembered the mother who had laughed often, light filling her face. And they remembered when she was gone, stolen from them, leaving them with the mother who had been a semblance of her former self. Despite her best efforts, the younger three had gotten the Norris Jean who'd been broken and shattered, their memories of her dark and tainted.

Noah had wanted to know their father more than Naomi ever had. He'd searched him out once, only to have the door slammed in his face, Nolan refusing to even meet with him. Nolan hurting her big brother had only further fueled her hatred for the man. She'd believed Norris Jean when her mother had said that he was evil incarnate and lower than scum. Naomi saw him as a sperm donor and very little else. Now he wanted to take something else from her, without even knowing she wanted it. Not knowing Naomi would do everything in her power to keep him from it.

She twisted a dreadlock around her index finger. She needed to make an appointment with her stylist to have her hair conditioned and the new growth twisted. She moved to the oversize mirror above the dresser, staring at her reflection. For a woman who'd recently turned thirty-six she didn't look half-bad, she thought. Her complexion was crystal, not one blemish marring her skin. She had a natural glow that made makeup unnecessary and she attributed that to her organic diet. She wasn't supermodel stunning like her sister, Natalie, but she didn't look half-bad, she decided as she suddenly found herself wondering what Patrick O'Brien might have thought about her. Had he found her attractive? Did he like her dreadlocks? Would he like her?

She gave herself a mental scolding. She couldn't afford to be distracted by any man. Especially a man who probably hadn't given her a second thought. Thinking about dinners and dancing and dating wasn't something she had time for with anyone. Imagining a man in her life, fantasizing about finding love and lust, was a luxury she couldn't afford. Besides, she had a business she was building, and despite wanting to expand that business into Utah, her life was in Arizona. Patrick O'Brien's life was here in Salt Lake City. It wouldn't work in any case, and luckily, she didn't want it to. Or did she? She released another sigh, the question spinning with a vengeance through her mind.

Brushing the thoughts aside, she took one last look at her reflection and turned in the direction of the bathroom, suddenly desperate for a cold shower.

Chapter 3

It was going to be a long day. And not an exceptionally easy one. Patrick O'Brien needed to run and he needed to get it done and out of the way before heading into the office. After his day started, he wasn't sure when he'd get another opportunity and it had been a week since he'd last worked out. As he stepped out into the early-morning air he took a deep inhalation of oxygen. It was just minutes from daybreak and a promise of nonstop sunshine and extreme heat. The weatherman was predicting triple-digit temperatures with a zero percent chance of precipitation. It was already warm and uncomfortable and was only going to get worse. For a moment, he considered driving his car to the gym and running on the treadmill, but he needed more than that and he needed to sweat.

He started out at a slow jog, circling his downtown neighborhood. His South Temple address was mere minutes from the City Creek Center, a retail, office and residential development spread over twenty-plus acres of prime Salt Lake City real estate. The luxury high-rise where he resided was one of the many new buildings, refurbished office towers and retail space that had brought a lively and diverse vibe to the city.

Born and raised in Miami, he'd found his move to the state of Utah had come with some challenges. Being far from his family was lonely at times, but when the chance had come to head the Perry Group's legal department, he hadn't been able to let the opportunity pass him by. His association with the Perry family came through his friendship with Garrison Perry. The two had been roommates, both graduating from Brigham Young University.

Freshman year, Patrick had been one of only a handful of minority students, and most students he met were surprised that he was there on an academic scholarship. Weary of the assumption that he must have been recruited for the basketball team, he found Garrison's invitation to go play hoops with a group of his friends hitting him the wrong way. The two had bumped heads, hard, almost coming to blows. Both were ready to change roommates when an astute resident advisor pulled them aside and insisted they mediate their issues. Working through their personal biases had come with a challenge or two, but then, before either realized it, they'd become the best of friends. Patrick had no siblings and he and Garrison both referred to each other as brothers from another mother.

This was going to be a big day for his best buddy. Since assuming the reins for the family business, this would be his first major project without his father's input. Since forever, Nolan Perry had been a stern taskmaster, never quite letting go, his hands somewhere in the mix of everything going on at the Perry Group. But this time he'd sworn to stand back and let Garrison rise or fall all on his own. Determined to prove himself worthy, Garrison was set on making his father proud.

Understanding completely, Patrick was committed to helping his friend make that happen. His thoughts suddenly flew to the exquisite woman who would be at the auction…and who wanted the land as much as Garrison did. She was going to be highly disappointed, and that thought suddenly pierced Patrick's spirit.

He came to an abrupt stop not far from the Starbucks on Main Street, his hands on his hips, his breathing slightly labored. Naomi Stallion was going to be disappointed. The finality of that had him off-kilter. He didn't know how deep her pockets were, but he couldn't imagine she could keep up with the bankroll the Perry Group had their hands on. Garrison wanted that property and Patrick didn't imagine him holding back. His friend had a selfish streak and he didn't like to lose.

Patrick blew out a soft sigh. He hadn't been able to get Naomi Stallion out of his head since meeting her. Those few minutes in her presence had him intrigued, and he wanted to know more. A Google search hadn't turned up anything about her. No Facebook or Twitter page to follow. Nothing about her farm or her business.

In his mind, she was like a brand-new book, waiting to be explored and devoured. Everything about her was intriguing, like a new language to be learned and appreciated, with the promise of a happy ending. She was that sweet discovery on the top shelf in the back of the bookstore and he wanted to study her, to uncover the nuances that lay between the lines.

A woman suddenly brushed by him, bumping him slightly and pulling him from his thoughts. "Excuse me," she said, juggling the cup of coffee in her hand. Her blue eyes shimmered, and her long auburn hair curled past her shoulders. Her expression was curious and inviting, and though there was once a time when he might have taken the bait, right then he wasn't falling for it.

"I'm so sorry," he said, stepping to the side and out of the way.

She smiled, stopping in her tracks as she eyed him curiously. "Beautiful morning, isn't it?" she said, in an attempt to draw him into conversation.

"It is," he responded. "Have a nice day." And he turned abruptly and resumed his run, thoughts of Naomi Stallion chasing after him.

Patrick O'Brien was standing just inside the doorway of the Cushman and Wakefield offices. His imposing stature caught Naomi off guard and made her breath hitch. Although she had expected him to be there, seeing him so suddenly had her nerves frazzled, and she couldn't begin to explain why. He wore a designer suit that fitted him like a second skin. He looked different from how he had the other day, in the gray silk jacket, white dress shirt and paisley-printed necktie. His shoulders were pulled back even straighter, pushing his broad chest forward more and complementing his narrow waist and long legs. His shoes were polished to a high sheen and his silky curls had been tamed with a fresh haircut. His stance was majestic and he commanded attention. As she looked around, she saw there wasn't anyone in the room who wasn't giving him his due.

Naomi turned swiftly, hiding behind her brother's large frame. She suddenly regretted not having gone home to change out of the denim coveralls she wore into something more feminine. The dress she'd considered still lay across the foot of her bed, matching sandals kicked beneath a chair. She brushed her hands over her cheeks, praying that there wasn't a speck of farm dirt or dust looking like bad makeup on her face.

Noah eyed her anxiously. "Are you okay?"

She nodded, looking past his shoulder toward the other side of the room. "Yeah. I'm fine," she snapped, everything about her expression saying otherwise.

Noah turned to see where she was staring, and burst out laughing. He shook his head, chuckling warmly. "Get it together, little sister. You can't afford to fall apart now," he said.

"I'm fine!" she snapped again. "Just anxious for this to be over so I can get back to work."

Her brother nodded. "What can I do to help?"

She lifted her eyes to his. "Pray," she said. "Just pray."

When the auction started, Naomi pushed her way to the front of the crowd. She clutched the numbered bid paddle so tightly that her hand had begun to cramp and her fingers turn white from the restricted blood flow. She shot a look in Patrick's direction and found him eyeing her with a warm smile. She gave him a slight smile back, then shifted her eyes away. He'd tried a few times to get her attention and draw her into conversation, but she'd gone out of her way to avoid him. She didn't need the distraction. She needed to be focused now more than ever.

A sudden commotion at the door drew everyone's attention. Turning to look, Naomi was shocked to see the renowned Nolan Perry and his son enter the room. Both glanced quickly about, then moved to where Patrick was standing. The trio spoke in hushed tones and then the two newcomers moved to the back of the room to hold up the wall, their arms crossed over their chests. Patrick shot another look in her direction and smiled, his expression almost consoling. Naomi felt herself bristle and then her body began to shake, her knees threatening to give out beneath her. Her brother's strong hand pressing tightly against her shoulder was the only thing that kept her standing.

Noah spoke, his voice controlled and even. "It's okay, Naomi. You knew this was a possibility." He gave her shoulder another light squeeze.

Naomi nodded, tapping his hand with her own.

The auctioneer called for everyone's attention, announcing the start of the auction. There was a brief description of the lot up for sale and then it started. "We will open the bidding at one hundred thousand dollars," he said.

Naomi lifted her paddle and gave the man a slight nod.

"I have one hundred. Do I hear one twenty-five?"

Someone else answered the call. "One twenty-five."

Patrick countered. "One fifty."

"Two hundred thousand," Naomi called, cutting a quick glance in his direction.

"Two fifty," he responded.

Naomi took a quick breath and held it. That land had been appraised at just over one million dollars. She had no desire to see the bidding go that high, but something told her with the Perry Group in the mix she wasn't going to have much choice. She blew the air she'd been holding past her lips and countered, "Three hundred thousand."

The back-and-forth intensified. By the time the bidding hit eight hundred thousand dollars, Naomi and Patrick were the only two still in the game. Garrison had moved to the other man's side, urging him on. With each bid she countered, he glared in her direction and Naomi glared back.

She felt her heartbeat quicken, and her chest tightened with a vengeance when Patrick bid one million dollars for the land they both wanted. He turned, contrition painting his expression as he waved his bid paddle in the air. Naomi bit down on her bottom lip as everyone waited to see what she was going to do. Her budget had been blown at seven hundred and fifty thousand dollars. To go any higher would mean a total reevaluation of her business plan and the productivity her current farms would have to be able to make up the difference. She calculated and recalculated the numbers in her head, with nothing adding up the way she needed it to. She suddenly wanted to cry and had to bat her lashes fervently to hold the tears at bay.

Noah suddenly leaned in to whisper in her ear. "Bid," he said, as he held out his cell phone for her to read the text messages on the screen.

A series of responses had come in back-to-back, answering Noah's message for help. Each of her siblings, and her Texas cousins, billionaires John and Mark Stallion, had pledged their support, promising to help with any shortfall if she needed it. Money wasn't going to be a problem if she didn't want it to be.

"One million going once. Going twice…" The auctioneer's voice echoed through the room.

"One point five million!" Naomi chimed. She crossed her arms over her chest as she turned to give Patrick a look.

The man's eyes widened. Garrison Perry inched forward, the resulting terse exchange seeming heated. Nolan had joined the two men, eyeing her and her brother with sudden interest. His unwelcome, intense stare sent a shiver up Naomi's spine.

The auctioneer paused before continuing. "Going once… Going twice…"

Garrison nudged Patrick's arm, but the man didn't budge, his gaze still locked on Naomi's face. When the auctioneer cried, "Sold to the highest bidder," and slammed his gavel on the wood podium, Patrick smiled, his grin widening into a chasm of gleaming white teeth. Beside him, Garrison threw up his hands in frustration.

Naomi jumped up and down excitedly, then threw herself into her big brother's arms. Noah hugged her tightly, planting a kiss on the top of her head. "Congratulations!" he said. "Now you need to figure out how to pay everybody back!"

Naomi laughed. "Don't worry. I have a plan," she said. "At least I think I do."

Patrick moved to her side, his hand extended. "Congratulations," he said softly. "You were a formidable opponent."

"You hesitated," she said. "Why didn't you bid? Clearly your employer is not happy right now." She gestured toward the Perry family with her eyes. Garrison looked like he was ready to kill somebody, his father standing like a stone as his son ranted.

Patrick tossed a look over his shoulder, then turned back to her. A moment of silence stretched between them before he answered. "You needed that land more than they did," he said, his beautiful smile returning. "Congratulations again."

He turned to go, then hesitated once more. His ego had been slightly bruised before; no woman had ever dismissed him the way she had. He'd been taken aback by her aloofness, but he refused to let that deter him now. "Naomi, would you have dinner with me?" he suddenly asked.

Behind him, Garrison called his name, his condescending tone grating on Naomi's nerves. Patrick tossed another look over his shoulder. "I said I'd be there in a minute," he answered, his own tone just as abrupt.

He turned back to her. "Sorry about that. My friend can be a little rude at times. I apologize for his behavior."

"Your friend?"

"Garrison Perry. We graduated from Brigham Young together."

Naomi nodded, and a gray cloud seemed to cross her expression as she looked from one man to the other, before her gaze settled back on Patrick.

He continued, "So about dinner. Maybe we can get together tomorrow night, or later this week, if you're available? I'd really like it if we could get to know each other better."

Her gaze skated over his face. His eyes pulled at her, with something in their depths almost beseeching. She felt her stomach do a flip and a wave of anxiety wash through her. But then she found herself nodding again, her head moving of its own volition. "I think I'd like that," she said.

Patrick passed her his cell phone. "If I can get your number," he said, "I'll call you and we can firm up our plans later."

Her head still moving, Naomi accessed his phone directory and pushed the add button. When her name and number had been saved to the device she passed it back to him.

He handed her his business card. "My private number is on the back. Just so you recognize it when I call," he said.

"Thank you," Naomi finally responded.

Patrick grinned wider and then, with a wink, moved back across the room, turning his attention to the two men who stood eyeing them curiously.

"The land you wanted and a date!" Noah exclaimed, stepping up behind her. "Sounds like today was your lucky day!"

"Why didn't you counter her last bid?" Garrison snapped, the look he gave Patrick cutting.

Patrick shook his head. "You didn't want to go that high, remember? You specifically instructed me to go no higher than one million dollars."

"No, I told you I didn't want to *pay* more than a million dollars, but that I didn't want to lose that land, either."

"Well, it's done now. We'll just proceed with your plan B. This isn't the only land in town. I think that property off the highway would be better suited for what you want to do, anyway."

"And do you have a plan B?" Nolan Perry suddenly interjected, moving between the two men.

Patrick found himself feeling some kind of way as the older man looked from him and then to his son for an answer. His face flushed with color as neither answered, waiting for the other to reply.

Nolan shook his head. "Patrick, who is that young woman you were talking to?" he suddenly asked.

Their collective gazes followed Naomi as she exited the room, her brother following closely on her heels. Patrick replied, "Her name's Naomi. Naomi Stallion. And that's her brother, Noah Stallion."

Nolan nodded. He shot his son one last look and then turned and walked out of the room.

Naomi stood off to the side, a stack of paperwork and a paid receipt for the land she now owned in her hand. She was waiting patiently for Noah to come out of the men's room when Nolan Perry suddenly appeared at her side. She bristled, immediately feeling out of sorts at having her father close enough to reach out and touch.

"Congratulations," he said. "That was nice work in there."

Naomi didn't answer, her mouth suddenly dry, her throat feeling as if she'd taken a punch to her gut.

The man continued. "Do you know who I am?" he asked, as he rocked back and forth on his heels, his hands clutched together in front of him.

Naomi took a deep breath. "Do you know who *I* am?" she answered.

He turned to face her and was now standing directly in front of her. He wasn't at all how she remembered him. He was shorter, no longer as physically fit as the man she recalled. His hair was more salt than pepper, age having clearly caught up with him. His suit was expensive and his hands well manicured. His skin was tanned, as if he spent much time on a tropical island or in a tanning booth. With his chiseled features, he reminded her of the actor George Hamilton. Money, and a great plastic surgeon, had served him well.

"You look exactly like your mother. Just as beautiful," Nolan stated.

He stretched out his hand, as if he wanted to trail his fingers along her cheek. Naomi bristled and stepped back, shaking her head. Before she could respond, Noah suddenly moved between them, giving the old man his broad back. The chill in the air around them could have easily frozen hell.

"Naomi, is everything okay?"

She nodded. "I'm ready to leave when you are," she said, grabbing her brother's hand and holding on tightly.

The two moved toward the door and made their exit, leaving Nolan behind. From where he stood on the other side of the room, Patrick noted the tense exchange. Something wasn't quite right, and he suddenly had even more questions for Naomi that he hoped to get answers to.

Chapter 4

Patrick sat with his hands folded in his lap, his feet up on the desktop as Garrison rambled on and on about losing the bid at auction. Patrick knew his friend well enough to know there would be at least a dozen more auctions before he would be willing to let this one go.

"You should have countered. You should have bid two million dollars. There's no way she could have beaten that."

"You don't know that. And what if she had? How high were you willing to go?"

"As high as I needed to," Garrison snapped.

"So, you would have been willing to watch your profit margin on this project dwindle away just to say you won? Your father would have had a field day with that."

Garrison shrugged as he dropped onto the chair in front of the glass-topped desk. "What was his problem, anyway? He never said a word the whole way home. That's definitely unlike him."

This time Patrick shrugged. "You would know better than I would. He's *your* father, not mine."

Garrison shifted the conversation. "So, what's up with you and that Stallion woman? Why were you talking to her?"

Patrick's shifted in his seat. For a brief second, he thought about telling a little white lie, then didn't. "I asked her out to dinner. I'd like to get to know her."

"So now you're fraternizing with the enemy?"

Patrick chuckled. "Why does she have to be the enemy?"

"Because she beat me, that's why!"

He shook his head. "She's a beautiful woman and I'm interested."

"What about my sister? I thought you two were going to try to make things work."

Patrick glanced toward the ceiling with an exaggerated eye roll. Garrison had two sisters, Giselle and Georgina. For two years, he and Giselle had been an item, but Patrick had known early on that they had very different life goals. Like her brother, Giselle was selfish, and she could be very mean-spirited when it suited her needs. He couldn't imagine spending a lifetime with her. They'd ended things amicably, but he knew she held out hope that one day, maybe, he would change his mind and choose her.

"Isn't Giselle dating some tennis pro?"

"She's dating, but you know Giselle. She gets bored easily."

"Sounds like someone else I know. How are things with you and Barbie, Bridget, Brenda… What's her name?"

Garrison smirked. "Bridgette! She's a supermodel, you know. She's done *Sports Illustrated* twice."

"So how are things with you and *Bridgette*?"

"Things are good. She doesn't annoy me, so it works."

"Well, I'm glad for you. Which is why I'm taking Ms. Stallion to dinner. Giselle annoys the hell out me!"

His friend laughed. "Yeah, I can see that." He stood up, heading in the direction of the door. "Let me know how that works out for you. Maybe you can convince her to sell me that land for a profit. For a very small profit, of course."

Patrick shook his head as Garrison made his exit. He didn't bother to respond.

"It's not a date," Naomi said into the phone receiver, pulling her legs beneath her as she settled on the bed. "Okay, maybe it is a date. But it's not serious."

Natalie laughed on the other end. "You are so funny! When's the last time a man took you to dinner?"

Naomi laughed with her sister. "How old are you?"

Natalie's amusement billowed over the phone line. "Noah told us you start blushing and get all tongue-tied when he's around. I think that's pretty serious."

"Noah likes to exaggerate. To be honest with you,

I don't even know why I told that man I'd go out with him. I'm thinking about canceling."

"You like him, that's why. And, no, you will not cancel. You need to go have some fun."

"Still, wasn't it our mother who said all men are dogs and not worth the effort?"

"Our mother also said life is about living your dreams," Natalie said softly, quoting the words they'd heard Norris Jean say repeatedly while they were growing up.

"Live the ride!" both women chorused, remembering the quote their mother had cut from a magazine once. *Life is not meant to be lived such that we cross over well groomed and attractive, but rather that we slide in sideways, champagne in one hand, strawberries in the other, clothes in tatters, our bodies completely worn and totally spent, shouting, "WOO-HOO! What a ride!"* It was what Norris Jean had wanted for all her children. For them to live their lives with complete abandon.

Naomi nodded into the receiver. "Well, it's really not all that serious. We'll probably never see each other again after."

Natalie laughed. "Keep saying it and you might actually believe it."

"Why did you call me?"

"How are you doing after running into our father? Noah said that wasn't good."

"It wasn't anything. He spoke, we didn't. We left."

"I wish I'd been there. I want to know why he abandoned us the way he did. I would have asked him."

"I got the distinct impression that he doesn't see it

that way. He asked me if I knew who he was, like he was the Pied Piper and I should have been in awe of him."

"And you didn't say anything to him?"

"I asked him if he knew who *I* was, then Noah got between us and he and I left."

Naomi could picture her sister shaking her head. "Do you think you'll see him again?" Natalie asked.

Naomi paused, pondering the question. "I hope not," she said softly, but there was something in her voice not quite convincing.

Natalie allowed the moment to sweep between them, sensing a longing and a disappointment that she'd never heard from her sister before. She wasn't sure how to deal with it so she changed the subject. "So, what are you wearing on your date?"

Patrick had called her twice, and twice Naomi hadn't answered, though he'd left messages in her voice mail both times. He was starting to feel as if he was being snubbed and he didn't like it. He didn't like it one bit. The third time wasn't going to be a charm for her or anyone. As he pulled his car onto the gravel drive of Norris Farms, he was determined to alter that, to change her mind and ease any doubt she might be having about going out with him.

The property wasn't at all what he'd anticipated. The driveway led to a picturesque farmhouse with a wide front porch and colorful awnings. Baskets of fruits and vegetables were available for sale, and there was a quiet bustling energy that seemed to vibrate through the early-evening air. As he stepped out of his car, a robust woman with jet-black, waist-long hair captured in two ponytails waved at him, her smile warm and inviting.

"*¡Hola, senor!* If you are here to buy the vegetables, we'll be closing in a few minutes!"

Patrick smiled back. "Thank you. But I was looking for Naomi Stallion? Do you by chance know where I might find her?"

The woman nodded eagerly and pointed toward the fields behind the house. "Senorita Naomi is there!" she said.

Following where she indicated, Patrick soon found himself knee-deep in a field of strawberries. The succulent fruit was in varying degrees of ripeness, some bulging red and others varying shades of green. Their sweet aroma scented the air and he found himself smiling. Toward the back of the patch Naomi was bent at the waist, picking the reddest berries and depositing them in a small wooden basket. She wore denim jeans that were fitted through the hips and buttocks, with bell-bottom legs, and a peasant top edged in tan lace. Her dreadlocks were pulled back and captured beneath a slouchy, crocheted beanie. The view suddenly had him salivating, the round of her backside beckoning his attention. His eyes widened as he watched her, in awe at how quickly she was snapping the berries from their stems.

She suddenly stood upright, turned and gasped, clearly startled by the sight of him. "Patrick!"

"Naomi, hey! I was looking for you." He smiled sheepishly.

She clutched the basket of berries tightly between

her hands. "I don't… What are you…?" she stammered, obviously trying to make sense of the moment.

"I would have phoned," he said. "But since you aren't taking my calls I figured I would just make the ride out here and try to catch up with you."

"Oh," she said, her cheeks warming with color. "Sorry about that. I planned to call you back, but I've had a lot going on and…well…" Her eyes darted back and forth as he stared at her intently, amusement seeping from his stare. Naomi felt a wave of heat sweep rapidly through her core, and perspiration suddenly beaded in places moisture had no business being.

She finally let out a loud sigh. "This isn't going to work," she said finally, turning back to the row of strawberries she'd been picking. "I'm sorry. I should have just told you that dinner wasn't a good idea."

"Why not?" He moved in beside her, reaching to pick a few berries, which he dropped into the container she was holding.

She quickly glanced at him, then away. He was staring at her again, and the look he was giving her felt like a torch intent on doing bodily harm…in a very good way. She drew a swift lungful of air and held it, trying to cool the swell of heat threatening to combust her from the inside out.

He chuckled, still eyeing her as she pondered a response.

"So, this is pretty impressive."

"This?"

"Norris Farms. You've got quite an operation here."

"Thank you. It's been a blessing, and with the new

land, I can expand our operations and open a community food co-op. I'm very excited about that."

Patrick's eyes widened as he dropped another handful of strawberries into her basket, moving along the row of vines with her. "A co-op? Really? Will it be open enrollment or private?"

Naomi nodded. "Open. And there's a definite need for one. I already have a lengthy list of prospective members. My farm in Arizona has been very successful and I hope to duplicate that here."

"You have a farm in Arizona, too?"

Naomi snickered softly. "I do. I'm actually based in Arizona, running my first food co-op there."

"So, you don't run this farm?"

"I have a wonderful manager who handles the day-to-day operation. I fly in at least once a month, or as needed, to handle financial matters, some operational issues, and to ensure that things are running smoothly. I'll probably be here more as we start readying the new acreage for planting."

"So where does all the produce you harvest go?"

"The food produced here is locally sourced by several restaurants, some of the schools and a few grocery stores. We also donate a percentage to the shelters and food banks. The co-op will allow us to do even more to help the community."

Patrick grinned, noting the rising enthusiasm in her voice. Light shimmered in her eyes, and the more she talked about her business, the more excited she became. Her face was animated, gleaming with energy. Her hands fluttered between berry picking and story-telling, and she relaxed for the first time since they'd met. And so did he, feeling a level of comfort that he hadn't experienced in a very long time.

The woman at the front drew Naomi's attention, waving her arms above her head from across the way. Naomi stole a quick glance at the watch on her wrist. "Oh, shucks! It's past closing and I didn't give Marcella her check!" she exclaimed. She pushed the basket into Patrick's hands and headed in that direction. She tossed a look over her shoulder, calling out to him, "Grab my bag, please, and meet me at the house!"

She didn't bother to wait for a response, but sprinted across the field. Patrick found himself grinning broadly as he watched her, more intrigued than he'd ever imagined being. He grabbed the cloth sack that rested a few yards from where they'd been standing, and after slinging it over his shoulder, picked one last handful of ripe berries for the basket and followed her.

When he stepped inside the farmhouse, the two were just finishing their business. The woman named Marcella gave him a bright smile as she relieved him of his basket of fruit and disappeared toward the back. Minutes later she returned, passing him a large sampling of the fruit and some vegetables in a grocery bag.

"Thank you," he said, then shifted his gaze in Naomi's direction, his eyes questioning.

She gave him a smile. "You earned it," she said. "The beauty of a co-op is that you'll be able to buy produce at a substantially reduced rate, or even work for it if you want to get your hands dirty. I hope you'll consider becoming a member."

He reached into the bag, grabbed a berry and took a bite. "I don't mind getting my hands dirty," he said. "I'm going to look forward to it. Especially if you're here."

Naomi felt herself blushing, and found herself shifting nervously as Marcella sauntered to her car, waving goodbye as the two of them stood watching. It was suddenly too quiet, with just soft strains of music coming from the sound system.

"I owe you an apology," Naomi said at last, turning to look him in the eye. "I should have called you back. That was rude of me, and my mother raised me better than that."

Patrick met the look she was giving him with one of his own. Something had shifted between them, with Naomi feeling more like a good friend than a casual acquaintance he'd just met. "I hope you'll make it up to me by letting me take you to that dinner."

She smiled. "I'd like that. I'd like that a lot."

He peered down at his own watch. "I need to go shower and change," he said, waving his berry-stained fingers. "I'll pick you up at eight."

Naomi appeared stunned, a wave of surprise washing over her expression. "You mean tonight?"

His mouth lifted. "I can't risk you changing your mind." He moved toward the door, then paused. "Shall I pick you up here or…?"

"My brother's," she said with a warm laugh, impressed with his commanding spirit. "I'll text you the address."

He reached for the phone in his back pocket, eyeing it and then her. When he didn't make any motion to leave, Naomi laughed. She grabbed her own cell phone from the counter. Seconds later, Patrick's phone chimed. With a wink, he turned, doing an inner happy dance as he headed to his car.

Naomi took in her reflection, standing at the full-length mirror as she assessed the dress she'd finally chosen to wear. It was a printed tunic with a hemline that fell to midthigh. It featured button detailing down the front, with a V-neck and slight ruffled collar. The sleeves were long, with billowy flared cuffs. The dress was a gift from her sister, a design from one of the many fashion shows Natalie had been featured in. Its bohemian flavor was everything Naomi. She'd paired it with thigh-high, burgundy suede boots designed by Natalie's husband, the renowned Tinjin Braddy. It had just the right balance of casual and dressy. She'd coiled her dreadlocks around hair rods before stepping into the shower, and the steam had left the thick tresses with a beautiful curl pattern that cascaded past her shoulders. She'd used a lightly tinted moisturizer on her face, and completed the look with a hint of eyeliner and clear lip gloss. With a slight turn, left and then right, she nodded in approval.

Her brother's voice echoed from the doorway. "You look beautiful! Mr. O'Brien should be quite impressed."

Naomi turned to meet his warm smile. "Thank you. I still think this might be a mistake."

Noah shrugged. "Maybe. Maybe not. I had a ton of doubts the weekend of my high school reunion when Catherine and I reconnected. Look how that turned out!

This just might be a blessing in disguise. Besides, you deserve a happily-ever-after."

"You've really gotten mushy in your old age," she quipped, as she reached for the purse she'd tossed on the bed.

Noah laughed. "They say love will do that to you. We'll see what you're like in a few weeks."

Naomi rolled her eyes. "When are you leaving?"

"I'm taking the red-eye back to New York tonight, so I won't be here when you get home from your date. In case you want to invite your young man in for a nightcap…or something…" Noah laughed.

"I am so done with you," Naomi said, laughing with him. She pushed past her brother, punching him lightly in the chest as she did so.

The two moved down the hallway to the family room, where they each took a seat. Nervous energy caused Naomi to twist in her chair as she looked from her watch to the oversize clock on the wall and back. The big-screen television was on in the background, an old episode of *Law and Order* flashing across the screen.

When the doorbell rang, both Naomi and her brother jumped, the loud intonation surprising them. Noah grinned as he cut his eyes toward her. "So, are you ready?" he asked.

She took a deep breath. "As ready as I'll ever be."

He got to his feet and headed for the front door. Naomi stood with him. "I can get it," she said.

"You can also make an entrance," he quipped. "Guys actually like that. It's dramatic and special."

"Says the man who dated only his wife and one other woman in his whole life."

Noah laughed. "You say that like I don't have any experience," he countered, as the doorbell rang a second time.

Naomi giggled. "I think you forget who dressed you for both those dates."

He shook his index finger at her, then turned toward the foyer. Naomi twisted her hands together nervously when she heard Patrick's voice ring out in greeting. And then she heard a second voice that surprised her. Her brother was laughing, which didn't help to quell her anxiety. Seconds later, three men came through the entrance, Noah leading Patrick and a stranger.

"Naomi, both of these men claim they're your date for tonight," Noah said, his tone tinged with laughter.

Patrick and the other guy tossed each other a look. The man checked his watch. "I was told to be here at eight."

"So was I," Patrick said, curiosity seeping from his eyes.

Naomi felt her knees begin to shake as she eyed the short, bald man with reservation. "I'm sorry, but I don't know you," she said, taking a step toward Patrick.

The man smiled. "I'm with the car service. Someone is headed to the airport?"

Noah slapped his hand against his forehead. "My bad. He's *my* date!"

The three men laughed heartily as Naomi tossed her brother a chilly look.

"It was good to see you again, Patrick," Noah said. "You two have a great time!" The two men shook hands.

"Safe travels," Patrick responded. "And enjoy your trip."

"Thank you. I will," he answered. "Going home to see my wife!" He moved to his sister's side and gave her a kiss on the cheek. "I'll call to check on you tomorrow," he said. "And please have yourself some fun!"

Naomi nodded. "Love you, too! And kiss Cat for me."

The bald man gave Naomi a slight wave as he turned to follow Noah out the door, grabbing the luggage that rested in wait. When the door slammed behind them Patrick and Naomi stood face-to-face, suddenly self-conscious about being alone together.

"Hi," he said softly, his dark eyes brightening with his smile. "You look stunning!"

"Thank you," Naomi said. "You look pretty good yourself!"

And he did. Patrick had changed into a white linen suit, white dress shirt unbuttoned at the neck and black leather loafers. A fresh shave complemented his warm, freckled complexion and the meticulously trimmed goatee that adorned his face. The casual attire was classic and befitting to his personality.

He grinned. "Thank you." He tossed a look over his shoulder. "Your brother is quite the comedian."

"My brother is a master of bad jokes."

"I like him. And since I know I have to pass his approval, I hope he and I get to know each other well."

She laughed. "Wait until you meet the rest of the family!"

"That is my plan," he said, the slightest hint of arrogance in his tone. "And this is Noah's home?"

Naomi nodded. "It's actually become the family home since our mother died, but yeah, it's Noah's. He and his wife spend most of their time in New York, though. She owns Fly High Dot Com, an airline leasing company, so they're both back and forth. He is head of the company's security, or something like that."

"Wow! That's impressive. So, how many more of you are there?"

She shook her head. "There are five of us. Noah's the oldest, then me. The twins are a year younger than I am and we have a baby sister." She pointed to a family portrait that rested on an end table. The five siblings stood in formal regalia, joy shining in their faces. The picture had been taken a few months ago, when her brother Nicholas had gotten engaged to his wife, Dr. Tarah Boudreaux. The event had been a ceremony to honor Tarah's accomplishments in neurosurgery. It was one of the first family photos they'd taken after Naomi's brother had been injured in a football game and confined to a wheelchair.

Patrick lifted the framed image from its resting spot. "Hey, that's Nicholas Stallion, the quarterback for Los Angeles. That last game of his was amazing! We hated to see it end his career. So, he's your brother, too?"

She smiled. "Yeah, and that's his twin, Nathaniel. He's a doctor. My sister, Natalie, is a fashion model and designer. She and her husband live abroad."

"You're a beautiful family."

"Thank you. Do you have siblings?"

"Unfortunately, I am an only child."

"So, you grew up spoiled and rotten."

Patrick laughed. "Hardly. I was raised in a home with six cousins and a lot of extended family. Hard to be spoiled and rotten under those conditions."

"Where are you from?"

"Born and raised in Miami."

"That's where your family is from?"

Patrick shook his head. "My mother. My father and his family immigrated from Cuba and settled in Miami."

"You have Latin roots!"

"I do. I also have African American roots from my mother's side, with deep ties to the swamplands of Louisiana. I'm just a mixed bag of goodies!"

Naomi laughed. "Clearly! O'Brien is Irish, isn't it?"

He laughed with her. "It is."

"You know you'll have to explain that, right?"

"What about dinner?"

"We're still going, but I want to know how a goody bag of Cajun and Cuban from Miami got an Irish name. You have to enlighten me!"

"So, the short version…" He chuckled softly. "Pedro Lopez married an exquisite woman named Mariposa Fernandez and they had a daughter they named Alejandra. Alejandra fell in love with a reporter named Jack O'Brien, who'd come to Cuba to cover the rise of the Castro regime. Jack fell in love with Alejandra and married her. He also fell in love with Cuba and embraced everything about the culture. Life was good and they eventually had a son that they named Alvaro Lopez O'Brien. When tensions in the country became too much to bear under the strict reign, Jack moved his wife and her entire family to Miami. Alvaro grew up to be this strapping, handsome young man. He was a musician and played drums for a Cuban band. One day he met the most beautiful woman, Zora Hayes. She was an amazing jazz and blues singer with the voice of an angel. He fell head over heels in love with her, but she would have nothing to do with him. He chased her for years, and then one day, in awe at his persistence, she gave him a kiss."

Patrick held up his index finger. "One kiss. Days later Zora Hayes became Zora O'Brien, and they had one son—Patrick Alvarez y Fernandez O'Brien. And the rest, as they say, is history."

"Wow!" Naomi exclaimed. "What a beautiful story."

"Definitely one for the romance books."

"And I can just imagine the food you grew up on!" Naomi said.

He laughed. "I miss the food! I seriously miss the food. Do you like Cuban food?"

"I used to love it but I don't eat it anymore. I'm a vegetarian and I've actually begun transitioning to a raw food diet."

His eyes widened. "What's a raw food diet?"

"It consists of fresh, whole, unrefined, living, plant-based foods. So, I eat a lot of fruits, vegetables, some nuts and seeds and lots of leafy greens. Everything is consumed in its natural state, without cooking or steaming. I'm still transitioning, though. Not quite all the way there yet. But I hope to be fully raw and organic by the end of the year."

"And that's a good thing?"

"It's a very good thing." She giggled softly. "I'm a holistic life coach, and organic health care is very important to me. I teach people to live a healthy, happy, productive life, to thrive in their physical health and enjoy their emotional well-being in all their endeavors. The body is very important and what you put into it significantly impacts how well it functions. I can't teach what I don't actively practice myself."

"So, that steak house I was planning to take you to might be a problem?"

Naomi laughed. "I have yet to find a restaurant that didn't have some sort of salad I could eat. We can go wherever you'd like."

"But I want you to enjoy yourself. I want to make sure I can get a second date."

There was a moment's pause as they stared at each other in delight. Genuine joy billowed back and forth between them. His easygoing nature had eased her anxiety. She had grown comfortable with him and she liked how that felt.

"Let's make sure you don't crash and burn on the first date, Mr. O'Brien."

He reached for her hand, entwining her fingers between his own as they moved to the door. "No worries there, Ms. Stallion. None at all!"

Chapter 5

Patrick was a hand-holder and a hugger. Public displays of affection were second nature to him and he thought nothing of pressing a heated palm to the small of her back or trailing his fingers against her arm. And he held her hand. He held it as they walked to and from his car. He held it in the entrance of the restaurant he'd chosen, never letting go until he'd pulled the chair out for her to take a seat. Even during their dinner, he didn't think twice about reaching for her hand across the table to caress the length of her fingers. It wasn't the kind of affection Naomi was accustomed to, but she instinctively knew she could easily get used to it.

"So how did you come up with the name Norris for your farm?" Patrick asked as he lifted a forkful of kale salad to his mouth.

"Norris was my mother's name. Norris Jean Stallion."

"Now, that's interesting."

"Apparently, it was an old family name, but we didn't discover that until after she passed. That's when we found out we actually had relatives," she said, a hint of attitude rising in her tone.

Patrick swiped at his mouth with the cloth napkin that rested in his lap. "Do you want to talk about it?" he asked.

She shook her head. "There's nothing to say, really. Norris Jean wasn't your average mother. Don't get me wrong, she loved us immensely, but she really wasn't the maternal type."

"I'm sorry to hear that," he said, as he suddenly thought about his own mother. They talked daily and she was everything to him. Everything about Zora O'Brien was maternal to the nth degree. Listening to Naomi talk about her own mom made him a little sad, knowing all that she had missed out on.

"So, none of you ever called her Mom? Or Mother? Ever?"

Naomi shook her head. She shifted back in her seat. "No. She was always Norris Jean. She never corrected us and we didn't grow up knowing any better. It's just what it was."

"I'm sorry."

"Don't be. Norris Jean sacrificed everything for us. She worked two, sometimes three jobs to take care of us, and she was always encouraging us to do and be better. Being a mother was just a harder task than she'd been able to bear. Our father's rejection broke her heart, and it was a hurt so devastating that she couldn't bounce back from it. She loved us, but I realized once we started to leave home, living our own lives, that loving us from afar was much easier for her."

Patrick shook his head, empathy filling his gaze. "And you didn't know your father?"

"Oh, we knew him. He just refused to have anything to do with us."

"Excuse my French, but what kind of bastard doesn't take care of his kids?"

There was a moment of hesitation as Naomi pondered his question. She reached for her wineglass and took a sip before she answered, "The kind of bastard you work for. That's what kind."

"Excuse me?"

Naomi locked gazes with him. "Nolan Perry is my biological father," she said softly. "My mother was his mistress."

Shock and surprise drained the color from Patrick's face. He looked as if he'd been slapped broadside. His mind was racing and she could see the wheels turning as he struggled to find words to respond. He reached for his own drink and gulped a sip, then his gaze drifted back to hers.

"Nolan. Nolan Perry?"

Naomi nodded. "Yes. And he has never acknowledged me or any of my siblings. Ever."

"Does he know?"

"He knows."

Patrick's head was still moving from side to side. "Is

that why you seemed upset at the auction, when he was standing there with you and your brother?"

"That was the very first time we have ever been in the same room together since I was maybe…three or four years old. It was not a happy family reunion."

"Damn! Garrison never ever said anything."

"I don't think he knows. I don't believe Nolan wanted his congregation or his family to ever know about his black mistress and children. He knew it would destroy his image and maybe break up his happy family."

Patrick was still trying to take it all in. He couldn't begin to imagine the hurt that Naomi and her brothers and sister had been made to endure. He suddenly wanted to hit something. Punching Nolan would have made him feel better. He clenched and unclenched his fists to stall the anger he felt rising.

Naomi pushed at her food with her fork. "Sorry, I didn't mean to kill the mood."

"No. You have nothing to apologize for. I appreciate you sharing that with me," he said, as he reached out to clasp her hand.

She smiled, enjoying the sensation of his palm against the back of her fingers. A wave of heat trickled through every nerve ending, warming her nicely. "How long have you worked for them?" she asked, hoping to sway the sensations sweeping through her.

He gave her hand a squeeze before releasing it. "A few years now. Garrison and I went to college together, and after I graduated from law school his father offered me a job. I've been with them ever since and it's been great. Garrison's my best friend and we've had a blast learning from his dad and growing the business together."

Naomi wasn't quite sure how to reply to that, so an awkward pause settled between them. She hadn't anticipated him revealing that he was best friends with the half brother who'd been loved by their father more than her and her family. She was suddenly questioning if it had been a mistake to tell Patrick about her parentage. She shoveled the last forkful of her dinner into her mouth, praying that her expression didn't give away the doubts and anxiety that had begun to surface.

Patrick seemed to read her mind. He shifted forward in his seat, his eyes skating across her face. "Thank you for trusting me enough to share that part of your life with me. I'm sure that wasn't easy."

She lifted her eyes to his. "I've never told anyone that before."

He smiled. "I hope that you and I will get to share a lot of things with each other that no one else knows."

Naomi didn't respond, her eyes saying everything for her. She liked Patrick. She was eager to know him, to see where their budding friendship might go. And she did trust him, the intensity of that feeling surprising her. Needing to lighten the moment, she waved for the waitress's attention. When the young woman moved to her side, she asked about dessert. "Do you have a fresh fruit dish or sorbet or maybe an ice cream that's nondairy?"

The woman gushed. "We do! We have a mango sorbet that's wonderful. It's made here on-site and only has three ingredients—fresh mango, simple syrup and freshly squeezed lime juice. And the chef can easily put together a bowl of complementary fruit for you. Maybe pineapple, kiwi and a little passion fruit?"

"That's perfect! I would really like that for dessert, please."

"And for you, sir?"

"I'd like the chocolate fudge cake with extra whipped cream, and maybe a few berries on the side. Thank you."

Naomi smiled. "You know that's not good for you, right? You're clogging your arteries, elevating your blood sugar levels, doing all kinds of bad stuff to your body."

"So, you're worried about my body?" he said, teasingly.

She rolled her eyes. "I'm sure your body is just fine," she said.

"Sure? Or do you think you might need to check? Because it's perfectly okay with me if you need to do an exam!"

Naomi laughed. "Oh, so you have jokes!"

Patrick laughed in turn. "I do. But let's be serious for a minute. Tell me more about this organic lifestyle of yours. Can it really help this old body of mine?"

"How old are you?"

"I turned forty in January."

"Forty! You are old!"

Patrick laughed again. "How old are you?"

Naomi grinned. "I'm not forty!"

They talked for hours. He told her about growing up in Little Havana, the Miami neighborhood where he was born, and the winter jaunts to the Louisiana bayou where generations of his mother's people had lived off the swamplands. He was a mama's boy, excited to show off family photos and a YouTube video of his parents performing together. There were jokes about family dinners with tamales, gumbo and his father's beloved corned beef and cabbage. Patrick had grown up with music and laughter and a family who embraced everything about their colorful lives. All of it was a foreign concept to Naomi, when she reflected on the wealth of sadness that had always seemed to fill the four walls of the trailer where she and her siblings had lived. Things were much better now, and she was grateful, but she couldn't help wondering how different their lives might have been if the Stallion children had been as blessed.

The restaurant closed around them and then the manager escorted them to the door, locking it behind them. They drove around the campus of the University of Utah and through the downtown area, taking in the late-night sights. Patrick steered them past his highrise apartment complex. As they looped through the parking lot of Bountiful High School and headed back across town, Naomi pointed out the single-wide trailer where she and her siblings had been raised.

After another hour, Patrick headed back to the coveted Salt Lake City address she called home. Her brother's house was in Federal Heights, one of the most affluent neighborhoods. The homes there dated back to the early 1900s and the entire area boasted mountain views to the north. The house itself was a brick structure with a timeless design and modern touches. Patrick had been impressed when her brother had invited him inside, the well-designed floor plan offering effortless entertaining and main floor living options. From the foyer, he had noted the bold French doors that led to the outside. As he and Naomi stood talking earlier that night, he hadn't missed the marble surfaces, custom cabinetry and stainless steel appliances. The vaulted twenty-foot ceilings had given the space an inviting openness. But the more he discovered about her, the more he realized nothing about the place was Naomi.

"Do you think you'd ever come back here to live?" he asked, as he pulled his car into the driveway.

"I've thought about it," Naomi said. "I know that I'll be around more while I get Vitally Vegan up and running here, but I really like Arizona. I don't know."

They sat side by side, settling into the quiet. His radio played in the background, a soft jazz tune billowing out of the speakers. There was nothing uncomfortable about the moment, neither of them feeling uneasy or anxious. Naomi finally broke the silence.

"Thank you. I had a really good time tonight."

He shifted his gaze to meet hers. "So did I. I'm glad you gave me a chance."

She laughed, the warm lilt of it vibrating through him. "I'm glad you came looking for me. I really was ready to run. It's been a long time since I've dated."

He nodded. "So, I guess that means it's been a long time since you were last kissed?"

Naomi felt herself blush. "I can admit it. It's been a while," she said.

"Huh," he muttered, seeming to ponder her response.

She giggled, and Naomi wasn't a giggler. Color warmed her cheeks, tinting them a deep shade of pink. "What about you? When was your last kiss?"

"Honest?"

"I expect nothing less."

"Yesterday."

A rumble of jealousy suddenly flooded Naomi's spirit. The foreign emotion caught her off guard and she heard herself gasp. "Yesterday?"

He nodded, his smile widening as he watched her. "Mrs. Maher. She lives two floors below me. I stopped to drop off a package that had been left for her. The woman attacked and had me in a lip-lock before I knew what was happening. Practically needed a crowbar to pry her off. It scared the bejesus out of me!"

Naomi laughed heartily. "You are so not funny!"

"I had you nervous, though, didn't I?"

"No."

"Yes, I did."

"No. You didn't. It's none of my business who you might be kissing. You can kiss anybody you want to."

He hesitated for a split second. "Okay."

"Just okay?"

He shrugged. "Yeah."

She shook her head. "On that note, I should probably head inside. It's late and we both have work in the morning."

"I'll walk you to the door," he said, then exited the vehicle, rounding the back of the car to come open her door. He extended his hand as he helped her out.

The walk to the door felt surreal. A full moon sat

bright and abundant in the midnight sky. The air was still and warm, and just the faintest sounds of a neighbor's dog barking and a passing car broke the late night quiet.

The motion-sensor lights illuminated the front of the home, triggered just as they hit the walkway to the front door. Naomi fumbled in her purse for the keys, her mind suddenly racing. Anxiety seemed to resurface and she felt herself begin to shake, a slight chill causing a quiver up her spine. She took a deep breath and then a second. Patrick reached for the keys in her hand and unlocked the front door. He pushed it open, then took a step back as he passed them back to her.

"Thank you for a really great time, Naomi Stallion."

The slightest smile lifted her lips in the sweetest bend. She nodded, fearful of what might come out of her mouth if she tried to speak. She'd been debating whether to invite him inside or not, unable to fathom what might happen if she did. There was something decadent, full and abundant growing between them, taking on a life of its own. But it was only their first date, and she kept repeating that over and over again in her mind. She took another deep breath.

"This was fun," she finally said, emotion fueling her words.

"When can we do it again?" he asked. "Because I really want to see you again."

Naomi smiled. "I'll call you," she said, a hint of teasing in her tone.

Patrick's deep laugh echoed loudly. "Touché!" he

said, amusement filling his gaze. "You really plan to make me work hard, don't you?"

"I want to make sure you know I'm not easy and that I'm also well worth your efforts."

He nodded. "You better call me, Natalie Stallion, because if I don't hear from you, I will come find you. You know that."

She laughed with him. "I will! I promise."

"Good night, Naomi."

"Good night, Patrick."

He started to turn and then stopped short. Naomi's breath caught in her chest as he suddenly eased an arm around her waist and pulled her close. Her heart felt as if it skipped a few beats, then synchronized sweetly with the pounding in his chest. Their gazes locked together and his eyes danced with hers, and then he cupped his palm against her cheek, gently lifting her chin. "You are the only woman I want to kiss," he said softly.

Her tongue peeked slightly past her lips, moistening them, and she felt her eyes close in anticipation. Time stopped and then, with the gentlest touch, Patrick pressed a damp kiss to her other cheek, allowing his lips to linger there. The moment was surreal, feeling like an eternity before he pulled away. Naomi inhaled swiftly as her eyes flew open, meeting his sweet smile, and then he was gone, hurrying toward his car as she stood staring after him.

Chapter 6

Patrick wanted to call and tell someone about his date. In the past, he would have given Garrison a blow-by-blow account of what had and hadn't happened. But this time he had no interest in sharing anything with his old friend, least of all what was between him and Naomi. This date had been wholeheartedly different from anything he'd ever experienced, and he didn't want it marred by college frat-boy jokes and childish innuendo.

Despite his best friend's many faults, Garrison was exceptionally protective of his sisters. When it came to the women he loved, he earnestly tried to be a true gentleman. Now, knowing their kinship, Patrick didn't want to put Naomi in the path of anything his buddy would later regret if he ever found out the truth. Garrison could be crass about some women and not exceptionally sensitive. And if Garrison said something out of turn, Patrick knew it could become a problem between them. His being privy to Naomi's secret suddenly had him exceptionally protective of her.

He reached for his cell phone, pressed a number and waited for it to be answered. Three rings and his father's booming voice called out his name. A Leoni Torres song, one of his father's favorites, was playing in the background and it made Patrick smile.

"¿Hola, Papi, *cómo estás?"* he asked, greeting him in Spanish.

"Patrick, how are you, Hijo?"

"I'm good. Thought I'd call to check on you."

There was a slight pause on the other end. "You checked on us this morning, son. What's wrong?"

Patrick took a deep breath. "There's nothing wrong. I just…well…"

His father laughed, his hearty tone ringing through the phone line. "How was your date? You had a date, right?"

Patrick laughed in turn, suddenly feeling foolish. "I did have a date and it was good. It was really good."

"So, tell me about this young lady."

Patrick settled back in his leather recliner. "Her name's Naomi. Naomi Stallion. And she's beautiful, Papi. Absolutely beautiful!"

Minutes later he'd told his father everything he knew about Naomi. He told him about how they'd met. About the auction, her business and her connection to his friend and the man who had mentored him. He delighted in sharing the details of their dinner date and how she made him laugh. How comfortable he was in her presence and how he wanted to get to know her better.

His father had listened intently, asking a question here or there that he'd been eager to answer. When there was little else left for him to tell, he waited for his father to say something. Anything. But he wasn't expecting the question that came.

"What will you do if you have to choose between this woman and your friendship with Garrison?"

"Excuse me?" Patrick said, a wave of confusion washing over him. "I don't understand."

"If you and she become serious, and you must choose between them, what will you do? Naomi might not be able to come together and be friends, least of all family, with the Perrys the way you might like. What will you do then?"

There was a heavy pause as Patrick pondered his father's question. He hadn't considered that the woman he chose to be with wouldn't be able to be friends with the people he considered his second family. Suddenly that thought had him feeling out of sorts.

"Hijo, it's just something that you may have to consider if you and this woman become closer. If she becomes important to you, you very well may have to choose. You need to prepare for that."

With a heavy breath, Patrick answered, "She's already important to me, Papi."

Sleep refused to come. Patrick tossed and turned and finally rolled out of bed and stumbled through the darkness to the living room. He dropped onto the sofa and turned on the television. A late-night infomercial suddenly blared from the speakers, someone selling a miracle cure for stretch marks. He switched channels until he came across an old black-and-white Western playing on a classic-movies station. He adjusted the volume down a bit and settled back against the pillows.

Since ending the conversation with his father he hadn't been able to stop thinking about Naomi. He'd thought about calling her, twice dialing and then disconnecting the call before it rang on the other end. Feeling awkward was out of character for him, but everything he'd found himself feeling about the woman was out of the norm.

Naomi's nontraditional approach to life was intriguing to him. He understood when she said that her friends and family were often challenged by how she did things, but he found her youthful exuberance and her bohemian spirit refreshing. Despite her carefree spirit and devil-may-care attitude, she possessed an astute business expertise and she had just enough of a competitive nature to give any challenger a run for their money.

He really liked Naomi. He liked her more than he had expected to, and that fact had surprised him. She was not like any woman he'd ever dated. Women who'd been desperate for husbands and financial futures that would enable them to be stay-at-home, country-club moms. Women who wouldn't be caught dead in overalls, or get their hands dirty simply because they loved it. Women who were shallow and callous and so self-absorbed that he was more of a notch on their belt than anything else.

What he found himself feeling for Naomi also had him wondering what she might be feeling for him. Because he wanted her to feel something. He realized he'd be devastated if she felt nothing at all. He lifted his phone in his palm for the umpteenth time, debating yet again whether to call Naomi. With nothing to lose and everything possible to gain, he finally dialed, crossing his fingers that he wasn't making a complete and utter fool of himself.

"I knew I shouldn't have called you," Naomi snipped, as her sister laughed on the other end of the phone line. "I should have just kept the details of my date to myself."

"That wouldn't have been any fun," Natalie said. "Why didn't you just invite the man inside? You know you wanted to."

"I didn't want him to think I was fast. Or easy."

"But you are."

"I am not! I'm controlling, maybe a little neurotic, but any man I'm going to be with is going to have to work for it. I don't just give my very good girl away, willy-nilly, without some level of emotional commitment."

Natalie laughed hysterically. "Oh, gosh!" she gasped, fighting to catch her breath. "I haven't heard that since I was thirteen! Norris Jean would always tell us to keep our legs closed and our very good girls good. It was years before I figured out she was talking about our vaginas."

"It wasn't your vagina she was concerned about. It

was your uterus. Your mother had no interest in being anyone's grandmother."

"She was barely interested in being anyone's mother!"

"Exactly. You could use your vagina all you wanted as long as you didn't come up pregnant."

"So, you're really going to make this man work for your good girl?"

"It's the respectable thing to do," Naomi said with a deep chuckle.

"Oh, my gosh! You really like this man!" Natalie screamed loudly into the telephone.

Naomi rolled her eyes. "Of course I like him. I wouldn't have bothered to call you for advice if I didn't like him, Natalie. Would you please catch up?"

Her sister laughed heartily. "Just be you, Naomi! He's going to love you no matter how hard-to-get you play."

"I wasn't planning to play hard-to-get. Besides, it wasn't like he was really trying to *get* anything. In fact, he was quite the gentleman." She touched her fingers to the spot where Patrick had kissed her cheek, and felt herself grinning at the memory.

She changed the subject, suddenly wanting to leave the conversation about her date and Patrick O'Brien alone. "Have you talked to our brothers recently?" she asked.

She could sense her sister nodding as she answered. "I've talked to all three of them. Noah says he likes your new friend. That you two make a very cute couple."

Naomi ignored Natalie's comment. "Did he tell you he and Cat are thinking about having a baby?"

"He did."

"So, when are you and Tinjin going to start a family?"

"When you have sex with one man, any man, the same man, for a whole year straight."

"You are so not funny, Natalie."

Her sister laughed. "Well, if you don't ask me about my uterus, I won't ask you about yours."

"Deal."

"When are you going to see Nicholas? He sounded good when I spoke with him. He says he's training for some handicap championship?"

"He's doing a paratriathlon. It's a seven-hundred-fifty-meter swim, a twenty-kilometer ride on a hand cycle and a five-kilometer race in his wheelchair. He's very excited about it."

"He sounded happy. He and Tarah both sounded very happy!"

"They really are. She's loving her job at the surgical center. He loves his new gig with ESPN and being able to commentate sporting events. They are making it work and I'm so proud of them both. She is so good for him!"

"Are they thinking about babies? I wanted to ask, but didn't know if it's a sensitive topic for them or not."

"I don't think so. He told Noah that they're investigating in vitro fertilization. But he also said he wasn't sure if he or Tarah were ready for kids right now. Her schedule is still crazy at the hospital, and his isn't much better. But I'm sure when they make a decision they'll let us all know."

"Well, they shouldn't rush into anything. I know Tinjin and I are definitely not ready. I can see us now, forgetting the kid in Paris while we're in London working, or something crazy like that."

Naomi laughed. "I'm sure your husband would not let that happen."

"Well, I'm not," Natalie said with a soft chuckle. She changed the subject. "How's Nathaniel? Are he and that woman still together?"

"You mean is she still obsessed and is he still ignoring her?"

Natalie laughed. "He knows he loves that woman."

"I don't think he does. Our brothers are clueless when it comes to the opposite sex."

"I should probably come home to help. You and Nathaniel both sound like you need me."

Naomi laughed in turn. "I really don't need your help." Her phone suddenly beeped and vibrated, indicating an incoming call. She looked down at the device and her eyes widened as she pulled it back to her ear. "That's him. He's calling!"

"Who?" Natalie queried. "Who's calling?"

"Patrick. He's on the other line. Why are you so slow tonight?"

Natalie giggled. "Go handle that. Your uterus is dying to hear his voice again!"

"You're the one with the uterus issues. I'm just trying to keep my very good girl good."

Her phone beeped a second time.

"Girl, bye! Your good girl would be much happier

if you let her have herself a good time," Natalie said as she disconnected the call.

Patrick was just a split second from hanging up when Naomi finally answered the phone. The sweet cadence of her voice vibrated through the phone line.

"Hello?"

"Naomi, hey. It's Patrick. I didn't wake you, did I?"

Naomi shifted in her seat, tucking her legs beneath her buttocks. "No, you didn't. How are you?"

"Missing you and that beautiful smile of yours."

She felt her lips bend upward and her face flushed with heat. "So, you're that kind of guy, are you?"

"What kind of guy is that?"

"The one with the smooth lines who thinks if he tells a girl how pretty she is he can get her to fall for him?"

"Is it working?"

"No."

"Then I guess I'm not that kind of guy."

Naomi laughed warmly. "Thank you again for dinner. I really did have a great time."

"So did I. When can we do it again?"

"I thought I was supposed to call you?"

"I'm not a very patient man. I got tired of waiting."

"It's only been an hour."

"It's been three. By tomorrow you would have forgotten all about me."

"You really don't believe that, do you?"

"No, but it sounded good."

She laughed again. "It sounds a little desperate."

"You do that to me. You've got my confidence shook."

"I do not!"

"You've got me all nervous and tense. I don't even know how to act when I'm thinking about you."

"Maybe you shouldn't think about me then."

"That's not going to happen. I can't get you out of my mind."

"You're definitely that kind of guy!" she said with a soft giggle.

Patrick laughed with her. "I just wanted to hear your voice and to tell you again what a great time I had with you."

"So, what are you doing on Tuesday?"

Patrick's excitement rose tenfold, ringing in his voice. "Having dinner with you again, I hope."

"If you don't mind a raw, organic meal, I'll cook. Would seven o'clock work for you?"

"I'll be there."

Naomi's grin was canyon wide. Her voice dropped an octave as she murmured, "Good night, Patrick!"

"Good night, beautiful."

She liked him. Naomi couldn't remember the last time any man had her so excited, but Patrick had butterflies quivering with a vengeance in the pit of her stomach. He made her laugh and he reminded her of things that brought her the greatest joy: sunshine, summer rain, caramel candies, her farm and her family.

She enjoyed the banter the two shared, their back-and-forth feeling easy and comfortable. The ease of it all had her feeling out of sorts, unable to fathom any relationship that could make her so relaxed and secure. But there was something very special about Patrick O'Brien and she was loving everything blooming sweetly between them.

With the barest whisper of a sigh, Naomi reached to extinguish the light on the nightstand. She rolled to the other side of the bed, pulling the bedcovers up around her torso. Closing her eyes, she allowed her body to relax and settle down against the mattress. Minutes later, sleep pulled her into a quiet lull, embracing her steadily as she said a prayer that Patrick might stroll through her dreams.

Chapter 7

Patrick shuffled the last manila folder on his desk into a side drawer and then locked it with a small key positioned on his key chain. He stole a quick glance at his wristwatch. He had just enough time to run home and change into something more casual before his dinner date with Naomi. A wide grin creased his face as he thought about spending more time with her.

They had talked every day since she'd extended the invitation. A few times he had wanted to rush things, anxious to see her again, but he didn't want to appear overly eager and scare her away. But he really wanted to spend time with Naomi, to see her laugh again, to maybe hold her close if the opportunity presented itself. He thought about doing that and smiled.

The moment was interrupted when Garrison barged

into his office, immediately noting what had to be a cheesy grin on his face. "What are you so happy about?"

Patrick shook his head. "Can't I just be happy?"

His friend eyed him skeptically. "Do you want to go grab a drink? Jessica canceled on me."

"Who's Jessica?"

"A little hottie I met at the bar last night. She's a flight attendant and had to go fill in for a friend. She's headed to Toronto and she'll be back later this week. I'll get the goodies then."

Patrick shook his head. "What happened to you and Bridgette? The last time we talked you were talking about getting engaged."

"I'm still planning to get engaged. But I also plan to have me a little on the side when it's necessary, and Jessica was definitely necessary."

Patrick's smile segued into a deep frown. "That is so not cool. In fact, that's downright trifling."

"You should try it. You might like it."

Patrick shook his head emphatically. "One day that mess is going to catch up with you and burn your ass good!"

"They have penicillin shots for that."

Patrick chuckled.

"So, does that mean you're good for that beer now, or what?"

"Sorry, boy. I've got plans."

"What are you doing?" Garrison eyed him curiously. "What's her name?"

"I'm having dinner with a friend."

"I know all your friends. Which one?"

"She's new. Someone you don't know."

There was a momentary pause as the two men stood staring at each other. Garrison laughed. "You're seeing that Stallion woman again, aren't you? That must have been some good stuff!"

Patrick's expression hardened. "Don't be crass. And watch how you talk about her."

Garrison dropped to the edge of the desk. His gaze narrowed as he crossed his arms over his chest. "You really like this woman, don't you?"

Patrick didn't bother to respond, his eyes darting around the room to avoid meeting his friend's. He shrugged his shoulders. "I'm getting to know her and yes, what I know so far I really like."

Garrison rolled his eyes. "You're sleeping with the enemy. And I thought you were my best friend."

"You really need to grow up."

"There's no fun in that. So, when are we going to double date so I can get to know your new honey?"

"I'm not double dating with you."

"I'll bring Bridgette, and not one of my side pieces, since you like her so much. And I'll be on my best behavior. I promise."

"No."

"Well, I would hate our first meeting to be at your wedding. Or mine, since we're planning on being each other's best man. So, dinner and a movie with my girl and yours should happen sometime soon. I'm just saying."

Reaching for his briefcase, Patrick gave his friend

a nod. "Good night, Garrison." Exiting the office, he headed for the elevator doors, his buddy's laughter echoing behind him.

The ride home was cathartic as Patrick set aside the workday and got his mind focused on dinner with Naomi. His brief encounter with Garrison had left a bad taste in his mouth. He had often ignored his friend's womanizing ways, chalking it up to the adage that boys would be boys. Knowing now that Garrison proudly emulated his father's bad habits, and his father's bad habits had devastated an entire family, had Patrick feeling out of sorts. He found himself reevaluating what he'd previously thought would be a lifelong friendship. Wondering if it had finally run its course.

The short ride through downtown, with Tupac blasting through the sound system, finally shifted his mood, angst replaced with anticipation. He'd been looking forward to this dinner date since the invitation had been extended. Hearing Naomi's voice over the telephone was no longer enough. He wanted to see her, to be with her in the same space. His wanting had become the sweetest craving.

An hour later, after a hot shower, and his favorite Acqua Di Gio cologne splashed in all the right places, all he could think of was Naomi and getting to her as quickly as possible. He donned a comfortable pair of denim jeans, a casual T-shirt and a pair of Nike flip-flops. With one last glance in his full-length mirror to check that all was in place, he grabbed his keys and raced out the door.

* * *

Naomi julienned the last zucchini through a mandoline, watching the thin, curly slices fall easily into a bowl. Minutes later, she'd tossed the thin strips with a fresh pesto made of basil, garlic, olive oil, a splash of lemon juice and freshly grated Parmesan cheese. After sliding the bowl into the refrigerator, she washed up the last of the dishes, took a second glance around the room to ensure everything had been tidied up and took off her apron, to wait for Patrick.

Excitement teased her emotions as she checked the dining table for the umpteenth time and fluffed the pillows that decorated the living room sofa. With the dinner hour approaching, she finally poured herself a glass of white wine to calm the anxiety that churned through her stomach. She was excited to be seeing him again, and felt energy rippling like a current through her body. She paced from one side of the house to the other to see if she'd forgotten anything. Just as she thought about turning on the stereo, the doorbell rang, signaling Patrick's arrival.

After moving quickly toward the front door, she stole one last glance at her reflection in the mirror above the console table in the foyer. She pulled off the scrunchie that held her dreadlocks in a loose ponytail and shook the thick strands free with her fingers. She clenched her teeth together in an exaggerated smile, then pursed her lips. The lightly tinted lip gloss she wore glistened slightly and there was just enough color to her face that she looked refreshed. She took a breath, counted to ten and then pulled the front door open.

"Hi," she said, her smile bright and inviting. She

reached for his hand and pulled him in, closing the door behind them.

Patrick grinned. "Hi!" He gave her fingers a gentle squeeze as he leaned to kiss her cheek. His lips lingered just long enough to stall her breath and have perspiration simmer just beneath her skin.

"Hi," she repeated, her smile widening. "I'm so glad you could make it."

"I would not have missed this date for anything in the world!" he declared fervently.

She nudged his shoulder as she gestured for him to follow her into the living space. "Would you like a drink?" She moved to the counter and the bottle of wine she'd left resting there. "I have wine, water, juice. And I'm sure if I looked in all my brother's hiding places I could probably find a bottle of soda pop or two."

Patrick grinned. "I'll take whatever you're having," he answered.

"Wine it is!" she said, as she filled an empty glass. "So, how was your day?"

He nodded as he moved to take a seat in an oversize recliner. "It was good. Busy. I spent most of it reviewing contracts. The best part of my day happened about five minutes ago."

Confusion washed over Naomi's face. "What happened five minutes ago?"

"You opened your front door and smiled at me."

Naomi laughed. She shook her head as Patrick laughed with her. She moved to the chair beside his and sat down, passing him his own glass of wine.

"So, how was *your* day, honey?" he said, his tone teasing as he shifted his eyebrows at her.

"My days are always good. I was at the farm for most of it and then here to get ready for you. I'd say I had a great day, too."

Patrick gave her a slight nod. He shifted forward in his seat, his forearms resting against his thighs, his hands clasped around the crystal goblet. "Your brother and his wife are still away?"

Naomi nodded. "They're back home in New York."

"You must miss them."

"Not really," she said with a soft chuckle.

His eyes widened slightly. "I wasn't expecting that," he said. "You and your brother seem very close."

"I adore my brother. He's my best friend and his wife is an absolute sweetheart. We have a great time when we're together, but they're still very much in honeymoon mode. It's made for some very uncomfortable moments, being the third wheel in their home."

Patrick nodded. "It's a good thing we met when we did then. I'm going to enjoy being that fourth wheel you need."

Naomi rolled her eyes. She changed the subject, a slight smile on her face. "I hope you're hungry. I've been slaving in the kitchen all afternoon."

"I thought you said we were having a *raw* meal?"

"We are. I still had to prepare it."

He smiled. "Well, I'm very hungry. I've been looking forward to this all day, so I missed lunch. And skipped breakfast, now that I think about it."

Naomi jumped to her feet. "You should have said

something. Give me a quick minute and we can eat," she said as she headed toward the kitchen.

Minutes later they were laughing heartily as they devoured a meal of zucchini noodles with a pesto dressing, Bibb lettuce topped with a mango-avocado salsa and a raw vegan lasagna with sunflower seed pesto, sun-dried tomato marinara, cashew cheese and walnut sausage. Each bite was an orchestra of flavors and textures that were a sheer delight. Patrick was impressed and he said so. "This is so good!" he exclaimed as he swiped a paper napkin across his mouth.

"Thank you. I don't cook like this every day, but I get very excited when I get the chance to share my diet with others. You say raw foods and people instantly think it's going to be salad."

"I admit it—I was nervous. But I'm amazed at how tasty everything is."

"It's fresh. Most of the vegetables I picked from the fields this afternoon. And it's so healthy for you."

"I could never make something like a raw lasagna by myself. And I'm not going to lie to you…I wouldn't even try."

Naomi laughed. "It took me a year before I felt adept enough to try this. And it bombed the first time!"

"So how did you get started? And where would you suggest I start?"

"Start by juicing. Fruit and vegetable juices will give you immediate benefits. They'll boost your energy and immune system and they taste good. I have some recipes I can share with you. Personally, I can drink kale lemonade all day long, it's so good. Then really think about your diet and make a concerted effort to eliminate processed foods. Integrate more greens daily and buy organic. Just those changes will make a dramatic difference in your health. Do that for a while and then start trying new dishes until you figure out what works for you and what doesn't."

"Well, you've clearly perfected your techniques. I want to ask for a second helping, but I don't want to seem greedy." He licked his fork before resting it on his empty plate.

"You are more than welcome to seconds, but you need to leave room for dessert."

"Raw dessert? Really?"

She nodded. "Really. We're having raw chocolate cake."

Patrick paused as he thought about that. "I'm intrigued," he finally said, his tone less than confident. "*Raw* chocolate cake?"

Naomi laughed. "Trust me. It's amazing. You're going to love it."

"I do trust you. And if you say it's good, then I'm sure it's going to be great."

"Well, if it's not, I'll whip up something else special just for you. Something that's all fruit, with maybe a little banana crème fraîche."

"That sounds like you're trying to spoil me," Patrick said teasingly.

Naomi winked at him. "I'm just trying to lure you over to my dark side!"

* * *

Conversation throughout dinner and dessert was easy and comfortable as the two continued getting to know each other. Patrick asked questions and so did she, both storing the answers away for future reflection. He made her laugh, at times gut deep and bringing tears to her eyes. Naomi was at ease in his presence, enjoying every moment of their time together. She had him feeling giddy with joy, the emotion settling so comfortably in his spirit that it surprised him. Time seemed to fly by too rapidly, the early evening shifting to late night in the blink of an eye.

Patrick glanced down to his wristwatch before lifting his gaze back to hers. "I should probably be leaving. This has been fun, but I would hate to wear out my welcome."

"You don't have to rush off," Naomi said, her eyes dancing in sync with his. Her tone was polite, but there was a hint of yearning in her voice and the look in her eyes said she wanted him to stay.

A wave of anxiety flushed Patrick's face and he bit down on his bottom lip. "I wouldn't want to wear out my welcome," he repeated. He rose to his full height, his body tensing ever so slightly.

Naomi stood, as well. "I'm sure that would never happen," she said softly.

Something magical seemed to simmer in eyes as he met the look she was giving him. "You're being kind. Thank you for dinner," he said. "It was really good. And I've had a great time."

She nodded. "I had a good time, too. Oh!" She held

up her index finger. "I wrapped that to-go plate for you." She rushed back to the kitchen, returning promptly with a brown bag in hand.

He laughed as he took the package she extended. "So, begging for the leftovers didn't make me look too bad, did it?"

Naomi snickered. "Not at all. It actually did wonders for my ego that you liked my cooking enough to ask."

The smile he gave her was wide and warm, the tilt of his head ever so slight. A pregnant pause blossomed between them for the first time since his arrival.

Patrick shifted his weight from one foot to the other. "So, this is that awkward moment at the end of our date where I want to kiss you again but I don't want to overstep my boundaries. Since we're still getting to know each other, it might be too soon. And I would hate to get slapped."

Naomi giggled, her eyes shifting in a slight roll. "Do you often get slapped when you kiss a woman?"

He grinned. "Not at all. But if I kiss you it won't be like last time. It won't be a casual kiss on the cheek. Or a light peck on your lips. This time I plan to *kiss* you like you've never been kissed before."

"Well, if I'm honest with you—" Naomi shifted her weight, rocking from side to side "—this is that moment where I want to be kissed, but I don't want you to think I'm too forward. I wouldn't want you to get the wrong impression about me. Because I am *not* that kind of woman."

Patrick leaned to drop his bag onto the coffee table. He took a step toward her, closing the distance between them. As he slipped his arms around her torso, pulling her gently against him, she clutched the front of his shirt with both hands. His eyes danced with hers, their gazes doing a slow, easy glide together.

"So, what kind of woman are you, Naomi Stallion?" Amusement crossed his face as he waited for her to answer.

Naomi hesitated as she pondered her response. When she spoke, there was something in her seductive tone that struck a nerve, sending a jolt of energy to his core.

"I'm the best thing that will ever happen to you, Patrick O'Brien. And if you kiss me, you'll never kiss another woman ever again."

His face lifted in the sweetest smile. He found her confidence sexy as hell, and everything about being with her told him she was probably right. Just thinking about kissing her had him twisted in a tight knot, knowing that one kiss was just a taste of what he wanted.

He nodded. "Well, if you really *want* to be kissed, I guess I could. I wouldn't want to let you down," he said, his deep voice like the sweetest balm caressing her. His breath was warm, gently grazing her face with the faintest scent of ginger.

Naomi laughed. "Is that your way of asking if you can kiss me, Patrick O'Brien?" She took a deep breath, inhaling the beauty of him as her eyes lingered in the stare he gave back.

He shrugged his broad shoulders, his gaze never leaving hers. "May I, Ms. Stallion?" The edges of his mouth lifted, something decadent and enticing in the smile he gave her, and without waiting for her to answer he dropped his face to hers, capturing her lush lips beneath his own. One hand cupped the side of her face as the other pulled her even closer. The moment felt surreal. It was every bit the kiss both of them had imagined, and as his mouth skated gently against hers, it quickly became so much more.

Time dropped and rose like a roller-coaster ride, twisting and turning them both until neither knew if they were coming or going. It stood still, then shot forward like a rocket, the hands on a phantom clock spinning out of control. Adrenaline churned in Patrick's midsection as he kissed her, and then didn't want to stop. He pulled her closer, the nearness of her body inciting a rise of heat that threatened to burst into flames somewhere deep in his core. She was a dream come true, the sweetest fantasy realized, and he imagined that if there was such a thing as heaven on earth, then Naomi Stallion was the lock and key holding him hostage in paradise. He continued to kiss her, his mouth gliding like silk against hers. Emboldened, he pulled her even closer, wishing he could tear away the clothes that separated them, wanting to feel her bare skin next to his. When she parted her lips, welcoming his probing tongue, he tasted chocolate and berries and the faintest hint of mint, while heat rained through his southern quadrant in a firestorm gone awry.

When Patrick finally pulled himself away, they had been standing in each other's arms for quite some time. He gulped air, his breath coming in deep gasps. He clutched her shoulders gently, still unable to release the hold he had on her, his fingers lightly grazing the length of her arms. Her eyes were closed and she panted, her bottom lip quivering. He couldn't resist the urge to kiss her again, wanting to stop their slight trembling. He pressed his mouth to hers, one quick peck, and then another and another.

"That was very nice," Naomi murmured at last, the words coming with a rush of warm breath. "You do that really well!"

Patrick laughed as he finally dropped his hands to his sides. "That was better than *nice*. That was amazing," he responded. "And thank you for the compliment, but I have to give you credit. I couldn't have done it without you!"

Naomi smiled, opening her eyes to meet the look he was giving her. She wrapped her arms around her torso, suddenly aware that her nipples had blossomed full and hard, rock candy protrusions that pressed tight against the lace tank beneath her shirt.

Patrick took a step forward but kept his hands to himself, sensing that if he touched her again, leaving would be next to impossible. His fists were clenched tightly as he leaned forward to whisper in her ear.

"You were right. I never want to kiss any other woman again." He gave her one last peck on the cheek, and as he drew back, winked at her. He reached for his lunch bag. "Good night, Naomi," he said as he moved to the door.

"Good night, Patrick," she echoed, still clutching her upper arms with her hands. She moved behind him, pausing in the entranceway as he headed to his car. He turned, tossing up his hand in a slight wave, before he took a seat behind the wheel and pulled out of the driveway.

Naomi watched until he disappeared and then closed and locked the door. With her back against the wall she slid to the floor, drawing her knees to her chest as she pressed her fingers to her lips, which were still heated from his kisses. She would wait a few minutes, she thought, as she stole a quick glance at the grandfather clock at the end of the hall. She would wait just long enough for him to reach home. And then she planned to call him, hoping he would be missing her as much as she suddenly found herself missing him.

Chapter 8

His laugh was gut deep and tears misted his eyes. Patrick suddenly realized it had been too long since he'd been so comfortable, allowing himself to just be. Naomi had him feeling intensely relaxed and it had been some time since he was so at ease. He listened intently as she finished her story.

"So, there we were, five kids sitting in our neighbors' tree, trying to watch a movie through their back window. It was the best time right up to that moment Nathaniel fell and broke his arm. And every one of us was pissed that he made us miss the ending. We never let him forget it."

"Sounds like you all were a handful."

"We are singularly responsible for every gray hair

our mother ever had. We were a hot mess when we were all together."

Patrick chortled. The two had been on the phone for hours. The telephone had become a lifeline of sorts, connecting them to each other two, sometimes three times per day. They started their days on the phone and settled down for the night with further conversation. Neither could begin to imagine what it would be like if they didn't speak so frequently during their days, since their schedules made it difficult to see each other without some serious advance planning. But that needed to change, and Patrick didn't have any problem saying so.

"Are you free tomorrow for dinner? I need to see you."

"I have my inspection tomorrow for my organic license. I'm not sure how long that is going—"

He interrupted her. "Make time, Naomi. I really want to see you."

"You talk to me every day."

"I miss that beautiful smile of yours. And I can't kiss you over the telephone."

She giggled. "I was wondering when you planned to kiss me again. It really isn't nice to keep a girl waiting."

"You're the one who always has something to do. You work 24/7."

"I'm building an empire. Work is necessary."

"You have heard that all work and no play makes Patrick a very unhappy man, right?"

She laughed. "I am not responsible for your happiness, Patrick O'Brien. You're not going to put that on me."

"Like hell you're not! We'll have to agree to disagree there. If I can't see you because your schedule is a hindrance to our spending time together, and not seeing you makes me very sad, then you are directly responsible for me not being happy. Now, do better. Dinner tomorrow. I'll pick you up at seven."

"Fell down and bumped your head today, didn't you?"

"Six thirty then. I know you can't wait."

There was a brief pause before Naomi responded. "You're right. I can't wait to see you. So why don't you pick me up at six?"

"Naomi?"

"Yes?"

"My happy meter just shot up ten digits," Patrick said, laughing heartily. And then he wished her goodnight and disconnected the call.

Patrick had chosen Valter's Osteria for dinner. The Italian eatery was one of his favorites, with great food and a casual atmosphere that reminded him of the Tuscan hills he'd fallen in love with during his first trip to Italy. The chef was a friend and had gone to much effort to accommodate Naomi's diet. They were dining on a salad of tomato carpaccio, arugula, radicchio, carrots, artichokes, raw portobello mushrooms, bell peppers and fresh *burrata* cheese in a light balsamic dressing. She'd added *zuppa cotta*, a soup of cannellini beans, assorted mushrooms and truffles with her meal. He'd selected the *gnocchi all'arrabbiata*, homemade potato dumplings in a zesty tomato sauce, with his.

Their conversation was flirtatious and engaging as they sat sipping on glasses of an expensive Bordeaux. The day had been a good one for them both and they enjoyed sharing the intimate details as they slowly wound down.

"I was nervous about passing," Naomi said. "Utah soils are inherently low in organic matter and it could have posed a problem for us. The soil structure and water infiltration are exceptionally poor and it isn't easy to till. Thankfully, we already grow green manures, so that was a benefit."

"What's green manure?"

"It's a cover crop. Plants that are grown not for harvest, but for the express purpose of incorporating them back into the soil to increase organic matter levels. They help improve the physical condition of the soil, aid in the control of erosion and weeds and prevent compaction. We already had enough dedicated acreage to ready the new land with no problem."

Patrick nodded. "Well, I wasn't worried. I knew my baby knew her stuff. They couldn't help but pass you with flying colors."

Naomi smiled. "Your baby?"

He reached for his wine goblet and took a sip. He blinked rapidly as he answered, "Did I say that? I don't think that's what I said. You must be hearing things."

With a roll of her eyes, Naomi took a sip from her own glass. "A man with a sense of humor. How did I get so lucky?"

He leaned to kiss her cheek. "Yeah, how did you do that?"

Laughter was abundant, a natural by-product of all that was good and beautiful about their growing friendship. In that moment, both vowed to spend less time on the telephone and more time talking in person. Being in each other's company felt good, and although neither had said it out loud, being apart had begun to pain them both, a dull ache growing with a mind of its own.

Patrick reached for her hand and gently stroked her fingers. "I thought we could go back to my apartment for dessert. My mother sent me her new album and I'd love for you to listen to it with me."

"Your mother amazes me. She's like this Yoruba goddess, Jackie Brown superhero in a Tina Turner body with a Whitney Houston voice."

He laughed. "She's definitely a handful."

"I've been watching those videos you sent me and she gives me life! I just love her energy and spirit."

"She feels the same about you. She can't wait until you two can meet."

"Have you been talking about me again?"

"Every chance I get!"

Naomi laughed with him as she leaned forward and pressed her mouth to his. The kiss was heated, a light brushing of flesh against flesh that ignited a slow-burning flame within them. Both were grinning broadly when she sat back, breaking the connection, promises gleaming from their gazes. Finishing their meal, they chatted easily for a few minutes more, then Patrick gestured to the waiter for the check. As he did so, he saw the Perry family coming through the door, standing in wait for a table of their own.

Garrison was with his sisters, Giselle and Georgina, and their mother, Grace. Nolan Perry was nowhere to be seen and Patrick suddenly found himself grateful for that small favor. There was no way for them to make an exit without running into each other, and no way he couldn't speak when they did. It would be bad enough for Naomi already, but running into Nolan, too, would have made a bad situation even worse.

Garrison saw him before he had chance to warn Naomi, calling his name loudly from the other side of the room. Patrick shook his head as he locked gazes with her. "I'll just say hello and then we'll get right out of here," he said softly, passing his credit card to the young man who'd finally come with their check.

Naomi took a deep breath and then a second. "It's fine," she responded. She had stolen a quick glance toward the door when she saw him staring there anxiously. Garrison was loud and obnoxious, the women beside him seeming indifferent and annoyed in the same breath. She knew of his sisters, the reputation of the Perry girls preceding them. From their debuts to their socialite antics they were well-known in the community. But this was the first time Naomi had ever seen their mother. Mrs. Grace Perry had stayed out of the limelight, preferring to pursue her philanthropic efforts with as little fanfare as possible. If it wasn't for her striking resemblance to her children, Naomi would never have known who she was.

As Naomi dropped her cloth napkin to the table and rose to her feet, Garrison was suddenly at her side, the Perry women following close on his heels. The two men greeted each other warmly, bumping shoulders in a one-arm embrace.

"Naomi, it's good to see you again," the man said, staring at her intently. "Patrick didn't tell me you two were seeing each other. It would have been nice if we could have all dined together."

Naomi smiled, her head tilting slightly in greeting. "Garrison. Hello."

He grinned back as he gestured to the others. "Let me introduce you to my family. These are my sisters, Georgina and Giselle, and my mother, Grace Perry. Ladies, this is Patrick's new *friend*, Naomi." His intentional emphasis on the word didn't go unnoticed and suddenly three pairs of eyes were studying her closely.

Patrick had stepped closer to her side, easing an arm around her waist. He gave them all a bright smile. "Hi," he said, tossing the younger two women a look. "Hello, Mrs. Perry."

Grace looked from one to the other. "Patrick, darling, how are you? We've missed seeing you at the house."

"I'm doing very well, thank you. I hope you are."

She nodded, then turned her attention to Naomi, extending her hand in greeting. "It's very nice to meet you, dear. Patrick is family, so any friend of his is a friend of ours."

Naomi noted the row of diamond rings that adorned her manicured fingers as they shook hands. The woman was pristine, the designer suit and red-bottomed heels she wore complemented by her shortly cropped hairstyle, diamond stud earrings and meticulous makeup. She reminded Naomi of a blonde Audrey Hepburn, polished and exceptionally refined. "It's very nice to meet you, Mrs. Perry."

"Are you from this area, Naomi?"

She nodded. "Yes, ma'am. Born and raised."

"What was your family name, dear? I might know your parents."

Naomi shot Patrick a quick look before she answered. "Stallion. My mother was Norris Jean Stallion."

There was a split second of reflection and then a moment of recognition. A sudden chill rose like a damp mist between them, the tension abruptly palpable. Grace Perry's eyes widened, saline pooling at the edges. Her jaw tightened as she gritted her teeth, and one hand flew to her chest, a fist clenched between her breasts. The moment was suddenly awkward and everyone noticed.

Garrison eyed his mother curiously, his brow furrowed. "Mother? Is something wrong?"

Grace shook her head and waved a dismissive hand in his direction. "Norris?"

Naomi only nodded, feeling herself leaning into Patrick's side as his arm tightened around her waist.

"I was very sorry to hear about your mother passing. You have my condolences."

Naomi nodded again. "Thank you."

Grace forced a smile to her face. "Well, you two enjoy your evening."

Georgina stepped forward. "Are you two just arriving? Or leaving? Would you like to join us?" she queried, her eyes skating from one to the other. Her smile was inviting as she and Naomi eyed each other curiously.

Grace bristled ever so slightly. "Georgina, these two are on a date. I'm sure they don't want us intruding." She moved forward, wrapping her arms around Patrick. "Don't be a stranger, dear," she said as she pressed a kiss to his cheek. And then, to everyone's surprise, she hugged Naomi, pulling her into a tight embrace that she held just long enough to make Naomi uncomfortable. Stepping out of her arms, Naomi didn't miss the tears that teased the woman's long lashes.

"It was nice to meet you, Naomi," Grace said softly. She cut a glance toward Patrick and gave him a wink. "And he's one of the good guys. You've done well for yourself."

Patrick laughed. "Actually, I'm the one who's done well. Naomi is an incredible woman. I'm a very lucky man."

Grace smiled. "I'm very happy for you both," she said.

The hostess interrupted the conversation, indicating their table was ready.

"Enjoy your dinner," Patrick said, as Grace turned and headed to the other side of the room, Georgina following on her mother's heels.

Garrison slapped him on the back, his voice dropping an octave. "Enjoy your dessert," he said smugly as he gave Naomi a perverse look, licking his lips salaciously.

The look she gave him back said she clearly wasn't amused. She turned her back to the man as she reached for her purse, which was resting on the tabletop.

"That's not cool, Garrison," Patrick snapped. "Show some damn respect."

The other man laughed. He held up both hands as if he were surrendering. "I didn't mean any harm. My apologies, Naomi. Sorry, bro."

Naomi gave him another look, but didn't bother to respond.

"I'm still interested in buying that land you stole out from under me. Maybe we could have lunch next week and talk about you selling it to me?"

She shook her head. "It's not for sale. Not now. Not ever."

His stare was suddenly cold, his eyes narrowing into thin slits. "Everything is for sale for the right price. An astute businesswoman like you should know that."

"What I know is that you will never have the right price. Have a good evening, Mr. Perry."

Garrison gave her and Patrick one last look before he turned, clearly miffed by the exchange. Giselle Perry was still standing there, staring at the two of them. As her brother stomped off, she eased her way in front of Patrick and brushed her hand across his chest. The gesture was teasing and purposely disrespectful.

Patrick tensed, his discomfort obvious. He grabbed her wrist, halting the slow path she was tracing with her index finger. He took a step back, bringing himself shoulder to shoulder with Naomi.

"Have a good evening, Giselle," he said.

"I was just being friendly, Patrick. Don't get all in your feelings like you do. You really need to lighten up and learn how to take a joke."

"And you need to learn to keep your hands to yourself," Naomi quipped. "No one found that funny, so don't do it again."

Giselle tossed Naomi a quick look before refocusing her attention on Patrick. She watched as he grabbed Naomi's hand and held it, squeezing her fingers. With a toss of her hair she sauntered after her family, not bothering to say goodbye.

"Something I need to know about you and her?" Naomi asked as they gave the Perry family one last look and headed for the front door.

Patrick shrugged, the gesture nonchalant. "Giselle and I used to date. A long time ago. Well, maybe not that long ago. But that's been over for a while now. So, no, there's nothing you need to know."

He and Naomi stared at each other as he reached for her hand again, pressing his lips to the back of her fingers.

She smiled. "If she does it again I won't be responsible for my actions. I will break her face."

Patrick grinned. "You made that very clear. I'm sure she got the message."

"And I may hurt you, too!" Naomi concluded.

His laugh was gut deep. "I didn't get that message at all," he responded.

"You just did."

"Does that mean we're official now?" Patrick asked, as they stood waiting for the valet to return his car.

"Excuse me?"

"Does it mean we're boyfriend and girlfriend? Because I think we should make it official."

Natalie laughed. "And how do we make it official?"

"All you have to do is say yes."

She stared at him, a wry smile pulling at her glossed lips. They stood there in silence, gazing deep into each other's eyes. The driver returning with Patrick's car interrupted the moment, before Naomi could think of a thing to say.

Patrick's penthouse apartment could easily have graced the cover of any architectural and interior design magazine. The contemporary styling was a juxtaposition of minimalist decor, clean lines, stainless steel and a color palette that revolved around multiple shades of gray with hints of black and white. It spoke volumes about Patrick O'Brien the attorney, but there was no hint to be found of Patrick O'Brien the man.

"So, who'd you hire to do the decor for you?" Naomi asked, looking around the space.

"Mrs. Perry recommended someone she uses. She and Giselle oversaw most of the work. It's cool. Right?"

"It's *cold*," Naomi said, tossing him a look.

He stood in the kitchen, popping the cork on a bottle of wine. He nodded. "It's a bit…well… It's…"

"Cold. There is none of your personality in this space. You don't spend much time here, do you?"

Patrick laughed. "Not really. I'm at the office more than I'm home. And when I'm not here I'm hanging out somewhere with Garrison. You're right, there isn't a lot of me in any of these rooms." He shrugged his broad shoulders as he filled two crystal goblets, then followed her into the living room.

Naomi moved to the windows as he set both glasses

down on the coffee table. With the push of a button on a remote device, he dimmed the lights and engaged the stereo system, so that soft music floated from the speakers.

Staring out the floor-to-ceiling windows that looked out over the city, Naomi paused, the words of the first song capturing her attention. The songstress was singing about being a woman in love with an unkind man. Despite the loneliness of her situation, she was still hopeful that love would see them through.

Naomi felt herself swaying to the music as she listened intently. She closed her eyes and allowed herself to fall into the moment.

Patrick easing his body against her back as he wrapped his arms around her came as a surprise, and she jumped, momentarily distracted from the tune. He murmured in her ear to ease her anxiety. Heat wafted from his skin and the subtle aroma of his cologne teased her nostrils. She felt at ease in his arms, safe and secure. She allowed herself to relax against his chest, her buttocks nestled snugly against his crotch. They stood quietly together, savoring the nearness of each other as the music flowed from one song to another. Outside, the city lights seemed to flicker in sync.

"Your mother has an amazing voice," Naomi said softly.

"She does."

"Has she always sung?"

"Since she was a little girl. She used to sing me Spanish lullabies when I was a kid. Her singing always made me feel protected…and special."

"She truly has a gift," Naomi concluded as she spun in his arms and pressed herself against him. She wrapped her hands around his waist, her fingers pressing against the small of his back. She rested her cheek against his chest. His heartbeat vibrated gently, the rhythmic *thump, thump, thump* soothing.

Patrick kissed her forehead and then her cheek, then cupped his hand beneath her chin to lift her face to his. He stared at her, wanting to say something, but unable to find the right words. Their gazes slowly meshed and then he dropped his mouth to hers and kissed her lips.

"So," he said, as he pulled himself from her, "you never answered my question."

"What question was that?"

"About making our relationship official?"

Her mouth lifted ever so slightly. Her coquettish expression made him laugh as she lifted her eyes to his. "You already knew the answer," she responded. "I didn't need to say anything."

"Humor me," he said. "I need to be sure. I know how dodgy you can be."

Naomi laughed. "Dodgy? Really?"

"You forget that I had to come find you that first time. When you were trying to get out of going to dinner with me? Or did you forget?"

Her laughter rang warmly through the room. "That wasn't being dodgy."

"Then what was it?"

Naomi paused to ponder his question. "That was me being afraid."

He tightened his arms around her. "Afraid of me?"

"No. Afraid of me. Afraid that I would want you."

He sniggered softly. "And you thought wanting me would be a bad thing?"

Naomi stared into his eyes. "No, the exact opposite. I knew wanting you would be a very good thing," she said, her voice dropping to a soft whisper. "I just didn't know if I was ready for what that would mean and how it might change my life."

Patrick kissed her again, the peck on her cheek lingering for a moment. His hands danced the length of her back, coming to rest against the curve of her backside. He tapped her bottom, then gestured with his head. "Let's sit down," he said softly. He clasped her hand and led her toward the leather sofa.

When they were seated comfortably beside each other, Patrick shifted to face her, drawing both her hands between his own. He hesitated, a multitude of thoughts flashing across his expression. When he finally spoke, their gazes met yet again, and she eyed him intently.

"I'm not really good at this," he said, choosing each word carefully. "I haven't been in a lot of relationships."

Naomi nodded. "I haven't had much experience, either."

"Then we're starting on the same page. I'm hoping that you want to see how far we can take this as much as I do. And while we're on the journey, that we have a great time together. I would really like to see that happen with you, Naomi."

Her mouth lifted slightly, the smile like a sweet breeze. "I'm already enjoying the ride, Patrick. But I'll be honest, I'm scared. I don't want my heart broken."

"I don't want mine broken, either!"

"So, what happens when I go back to Arizona? Because I do have to go back. And soon."

"Then we'll do long distance. I can commute there just as easily as you can commute back and forth here. Being apart will just make us appreciate each other more when we're together."

"And your work with the Perrys?"

"It's my job. Running the farms is yours. When we leave our jobs, it will be about the two of us and nothing else."

"That's not true. You have a friendship with your employer that goes above and beyond it just being business. I'm not sure I can deal with that."

"I see that as a challenge, but not one we can't overcome if this is really what we both want," Patrick quipped.

"And is it something you want?"

"I want to continue what you and I have started. I like the idea of the two of us together and I want to explore that to its fullest. So yeah, it's what I want."

There was a moment's pause as they both reached for their wineglasses at the same time. Patrick took a slow sip of his, while Naomi swallowed a large gulp. He laughed, amusement painting his expression.

Naomi set her glass back on the table. "I can be mean," she said, her eyes skating across his face. "Like raging, crazy mean. Slash-your-tires, key-your-car-paint kind of crazy. It's not pretty."

"I really find that hard to believe."

Her head dipped slightly. "You have been warned."

Patrick laughed again. "Should I be scared?"

"You should just be mindful not to piss me off."

"I will be solely focused on making you as happy as I possibly can."

Naomi grinned. She shifted forward, reaching up to wrap her arms around his neck. She entwined her fingers behind his head and locked them together. Leaning in, she brushed her cheek gently against his. The prickly beginnings of a five-o'clock shadow tickled her skin. His body was warm, heat wafting from his pores. He wrapped his arms around her, drawing her gently against him as she let her weight push him back against the sofa pillows until they were lying prone together.

Their mouths met in a passionate kiss, tongues entwined and searching. Every muscle in Patrick's body hardened with a vengeance, desire bulging urgently against the front of his slacks. Naomi felt him harden beneath her, his yearning a thick rod of steel between them. His hands danced the length of her torso and then he grabbed the cheeks of her backside, pulling her pelvis to his as he rotated his hips. There was a rush of warmth that burst from the core of her feminine spirit out through every nerve ending in her body. The intensity of it snatched the air from her lungs, hardened her nipples, dampened her panties and left her quivering with anticipation.

The wave of emotion was more than Naomi could have imagined. A rise of anxiety suddenly pierced her midsection and she broke out into a sweat. She pulled herself from him, pressing a hand against Patrick's chest as she moved back to her feet. Her wineglass was empty so she reached for his, draining it dry as she threw her head back against her shoulders.

"What's wrong, Naomi?" Patrick asked.

She cut a quick glance toward him as she shook her head. "I just need us to take things a little slower."

He eyed her intently, but she avoided meeting his gaze. He took a breath and then a second as he stood up. Reaching for her, he pulled her back into his arms and hugged her tightly, then stepped back and held her at arm's length. "We can take things as slowly as you need to. I don't want you to feel like I'm pressuring you or anything."

"It's nothing like that," she said, shaking her head. "It's not you. I just…well…" She bit her bottom lip, then dipped her head, focusing on his Italian leather shoes.

Naomi didn't have the words to explain the emotion that was flooding her spirit. His touch had ignited something deep in her core. Something that felt necessary and perfect and completely foreign to her. Something that was amazingly comfortable and scary as hell at the same time. When she looked back up at him tears misted her eyes.

"I'm just nervous," she finally muttered. "I'm not a prude or anything. It's just…well…" She paused a second time.

"Are you a virgin?" he asked, the thought suddenly rising in his mind.

"No… I…" She shook her head vehemently. "No, I'm not a virgin, but I haven't been with a lot of men, either. In fact, I've only been with two and, well…" She took a step away, not bothering to complete her thought. "I'm sorry. I should probably be going." A single tear rolled down her cheek.

Patrick stared at her for a moment. He stepped forward, closing the distance that separated them. He cupped her face with both hands, his thumb brushing away the saline droplet. He kissed her slowly, her forehead, one eye and then the other, her cheek, the tip of her nose and then her mouth, pressing his closed lips to hers. His touch was gentle and easy, and everything about him put Naomi at ease. She relaxed as he pulled her close, enveloping her in his arms.

"You are an amazing woman, Naomi Stallion. And I'm glad you're all mine." He lifted her face to his and kissed her again.

"Even though I'm probably being silly?"

"Even though you're being understandably cautious. This is very new. I get it. I also know that we have all the time in the world, so there's no need for us to rush."

"Thank you," she said, the faintest smile finally pulling at her lips.

He kissed her one last time. "I'll walk you down to your car. And let's plan on doing dinner again tomorrow, please."

Naomi nodded. She reached for her jacket and purse. As they moved toward his front door, she called his name.

"Yes?"

"You're pretty damn special yourself. And I'm glad I'm all yours, too!"

Chapter 9

Naomi felt like she was seventeen again, when she and Marla Kincaid's cousin Jimmy lost their virginity together in the back of his father's Cadillac Brougham. Marla had been Naomi's best friend since forever. Nineteen-year-old Jimmy had been visiting from Los Angeles, an annual trek he and his family had been making since he was a little boy. They were still friends, keeping in touch via social media, yearly Christmas cards and Marla.

That late-summer evening Jimmy had taken her for a Big Mac and fries at the local McDonald's and then had convinced her that there was no reason not to come out of her panties for him. They were friends, neither wanted a serious relationship and both had been ready to see what all the fuss was about. With less than twenty dollars between them, a hotel room wasn't feasible, her mother's house was out of the question, and since that Caddy had a big enough backseat, it had only made sense to the two of them to use it.

Six minutes of foreplay and one hundred eighty seconds later, it was over. That night, when she'd gotten home, she had more questions than answers, still trying to make sense of the moment. They'd done *it* four more times before Jimmy had returned to California. It was a few years after that when Naomi experienced her first orgasm, and she had Josiah Butler to thank. Josiah had been the local John Deere dealer, selling the farm their first tractor. He'd been all kinds of wrong from start to finish, and keeping in touch with him had never crossed her mind.

Remembering the men in her past and thinking about Patrick had Naomi's emotions all over the place. She regretted having pushed him away, when deep down she had wanted him like she'd never wanted any man before. She hated that she was home alone, tossing and turning in bed, when she could have been sleeping comfortably beside Patrick, cuddled close in his arms. She sighed as she rolled from side to side.

Naomi had purposely avoided relationships, choosing instead to throw herself into her work. Truth be told, loving any man was the last thing she had ever wanted for herself. Her mother's love for Nolan Perry had destroyed her. Naomi had sworn to never end up like Norris Jean—bitter, angry and broken because she'd trusted a man to keep her heart safe. Naomi hadn't planned to go down like that. And now here was Patrick, equally determined to break down her fortitude.

She turned and wrapped her body around a pillow. Stalling the heat that always came when Patrick was near was becoming harder to do. He excited her. He challenged her sensibilities, and she imagined that if she ever allowed herself to lose control, there would be no turning back for either of them.

Patrick was on the phone, laughing heartily, when Garrison and Giselle stepped into his office. Neither bothered to knock before pushing their way inside. He had just called to check on Naomi, excited to hear her voice before his day got started. After apologizing again for cutting their previous evening short, she'd had him smiling, her snarky humor a delight. He hadn't fathomed that he would love talking to any woman as much as he loved talking to Naomi. Everything about her vibrant spirit lifted his.

He hated ending the conversation before he was ready. "What time do you want to meet for dinner?" he asked, spinning in his leather executive's chair, away from the Perrys.

Naomi's voice rang sweetly in his ear. "It should be a short day today. I expect that I'll be done by six o'clock."

"Then I'll pick you up at seven. Will that work?"

"That's good for me. I'll see you at seven. Have a great day, Patrick!"

"You, too, sweetheart."

Spinning back around, he disconnected the line and dropped the receiver back onto its hook. Garrison eyed him smugly. Giselle looked like she was about to spit nails as she dropped into an empty seat. His gaze shifted from one to the other and then he shook his head.

"Good morning. To what do I owe this pleasure?" he asked, his eyes meeting Giselle's.

"We didn't mean to interrupt," she said. "Sounded like you and your new girlfriend were starting early."

Ignoring the comment, Patrick shifted his stare toward Garrison. "What can I do for you, G-man?"

"You can tell me how you plan to get my property back from that Stallion woman. I know you have something up your sleeve. How we can sabotage that stupid vegetable garden of hers and legally get away with it. I mean, why else would you be wasting your time with her?"

Patrick's jaw hardened as he clenched his teeth, biting back an expletive. He felt his lungs start to burn as he sucked in a deep gulp of air and held it. His expression was telling, ire building in his eyes. He glared, clearly not amused.

Garrison held up his hands as if he were surrendering. "Don't get yourself all twisted. It was a joke. Well, maybe not really, but don't be so sensitive about it."

"He's always in his feelings about something," Giselle muttered.

Garrison shrugged. "Seriously, though, I need you to talk to her. I'm still convinced that property is the best for what I hope to accomplish."

"Seriously, though," Patrick responded, "you are out of line. Your disrespect toward Naomi is starting to get old. I would hate for you and me to become bad friends because of it."

"Whoa, buddy! It's not all that serious!"

"It's not like she's one of us, Patrick. Clearly, she's nowhere near being in your league," Giselle interjected.

He snapped his head in her direction, his index finger waving. "Giselle, you do not want to go there with me. Why are you here, anyway? Last time I checked, you didn't have a job to speak of, and definitely not one with this organization."

"Check yourself, Patrick O'Brien. You don't want to go this round with me!" She crossed her arms over her chest, the gesture causing the too-small sweater she wore to pull even tighter across her breasts.

"Giselle, stop. Patrick's right. Why don't you go down the hall and see Dad or something while I talk to my man here? He and I are good. We're just going to agree to disagree. Right, Patrick?"

"I'm not going anywhere," Giselle snapped. She threw her legs over the chair arm, swinging them and the pair of expensive stilettos she wore from side to side.

Patrick rolled his eyes a second time. He shook his head, realizing his good mood had taken a quick nosedive. He drew a calming breath. "I have a meeting. Be gone when I get back, please." He pulled a stack of file folders from the center of his desk, stood up and moved toward the door, where he paused, tossing Garrison a quick look. "Let's do lunch. I think we really need to talk."

"No problem. Sounds like a plan."

Patrick nodded. "And don't bring the peanut gallery," he said, giving Giselle one final glance.

Garrison gave him half a salute. "Yes, sir. No problem, sir!" The man grinned brightly.

His head still wagging from side to side, Patrick chuckled softly as he left the room. Remembering that he'd left his cell phone, he turned back, then paused to eavesdrop when he realized the Perry siblings were talking about him.

"You need to do something," Giselle quipped. "You need to figure out how to get rid of that woman before she ruins him."

"Don't you think I know that?"

"Well, why don't we start with taking that little business of hers down? I'll help. Maybe that'll send her packing!"

Garrison laughed. "You are such a mean girl, little sister."

"I want Patrick back, Garrison. I want him to look at me the way he looks at her."

Garrison snorted loudly. "You drive him crazy, Giselle. You're never getting back together. Get over it."

"We could. He could love me again."

"Patrick never loved you, Giselle. You know that."

"Well, he could have. And he still could. He and I just need more time to make it work."

"Sorry, Giselle," Patrick interjected as he moved back into the room. "You and I are never going to happen!"

* * *

Driving home, Patrick couldn't stop thinking about Naomi. He'd been thinking about her since their call that morning. He'd thought about her at lunch with Garrison, and she'd been on his mind when he'd walked into Nolan Perry's office and handed in his resignation. Now he was trying to decide if he should tell her about his day or gloss over the highlights and not hurt her feelings.

Hearing his best friend and his best friend's sister plotting against Naomi had truly been the last straw for him. He couldn't begin to imagine how either had thought that was okay. Or could think that he would be okay with it.

He thought back to his conversation with Garrison. They'd met for lunch right after his morning meetings. Garrison had rambled on about his girlfriend, his side chick and wanting to take a guys-only trip to Santa Catalina Island.

Patrick had shaken his head. "You aren't really serious, are you?"

Garrison had looked at him with widened eyes, confusion washing over his expression. "What? You don't want to go to Catalina? We can always do Santa Barbara instead." He'd shoveled another forkful of tuna salad into his mouth. "Wherever you want to go, we can go."

"Why would you even think about trying to sabotage Naomi and her business?"

Garrison hesitated, his fork halting in midair. He finally dropped it to his plate and sat back in his seat. "I get that you're enjoying this little thing between you and her, Patrick, but I also know that you're a loyal friend. And loyalty is everything. To me and my father. We're your family. You barely know that woman."

Patrick pursed his lips as he shifted forward in his chair. "Family doesn't plot to hurt you. Family doesn't try to hurt the people you care about, either. Not any family I claim."

"So, maybe Giselle and I were out of line, but you know my sister," Garrison said dismissively.

"I thought I knew you, but I've been disappointed lately."

"What's your problem, man? Why are you making so much out of this?"

"My problem is you, and the fact that you just don't get it. I will not stand by and let you hurt Naomi. It'll get ugly between us if you do."

Silence settled between them as they stared at each other. Garrison gave him a slight nod as he tossed his cloth napkin onto the table. He stood up, throwing cash beside the napkin to cover the bill. "It's already ugly," he said. "I hope she's worth it." And then he turned and exited the restaurant.

Patrick sighed heavily as he steered his car toward downtown and home. Lunch had been bad enough, and then minutes after he'd arrived back at work, Nolan Perry had called, commanding a face-to-face in his office. Patrick had known by the man's tone that the conversation would not go well. Thinking about it made him angry all over again.

"Patrick, son! Come have a seat," Nolan had said, pointing toward the chair in front of his oversize desk.

"How are you, Mr. Perry?"

He had nodded. "Concerned about you, son! Giselle was here earlier and she's concerned that you might be in a bind. I was hoping to help."

Patrick had kept his expression blank as he took a deep breath. "I appreciate your daughter's concern, but she really should be focused on her own life and not mine."

"I know Giselle can be a handful, but I couldn't help but question if her concerns didn't have some validity."

"And what concerns are those?"

"Both Giselle and Garrison have expressed that your relationship with Naomi Stallion might be affecting your performance here."

"And why would they think that? Because I won't participate in either's scheme to tarnish the woman's name or cause harm to her business?"

"Because it seems that your loyalty may be compromised."

Patrick took a breath and held it for moment before he spoke again. "Mr. Perry, although I appreciate what I think you're trying to do, you're the last person who should be telling me about loyalty."

"Excuse me?"

"Doesn't Naomi deserve the same loyalty from you as your other children? Maybe even more, under the circumstances?"

Nolan had bristled visibly, his face reddening until he looked like he was about to explode. "Why would you ask me that?"

Patrick shook his head. "Your daughter deserves better, sir. Garrison and Giselle might not know Naomi's true identity, but I know that she's never done anything to either of them for them to think it's okay to treat her so abhorrently. You, on the other hand, do know, and you shouldn't be defending their bad behavior, most especially since it's focused toward one of their siblings."

"I'm not sure what that young woman told you, but…"

"Are you not her father?"

"I… That's not…" He swallowed hard, a visible lump in his throat. He shifted the topic. "I would hate to see us not be able to come to a resolution here. I can appreciate your concern about Garrison and Giselle's behavior and I have spoken to both. They know that I will not tolerate any behavior that is unfavorable to our business goals. What I need to know is that you are on board to continue to grow the business that employs you, and not focused on outside interests that would impede that growth."

"Mr. Perry, neither my integrity nor my job performance has ever been an issue. The fact that my personal life is suddenly cause for concern with you is a red flag for me. Who I date isn't any of your business, and it *definitely* isn't Garrison's or Giselle's."

"So, you plan to continue to see this young woman?"

"I most definitely do. I care very much for your daughter. Naomi is an incredible woman. If you took time to know her you would agree."

"You're treading on thin ice with me, son. I'd strongly suggest that if you want to keep your job—"

"I don't," Patrick suddenly said, rising from his seat.

"I can't, in good conscience, continue to work for a man and firm that I have no respect for. And I have no respect for you, sir. I appreciate the opportunities you afforded me and I regret that we have come to this point. But you really leave me no alternative."

"You're quitting?"

"Effective immediately. I'll insure Personnel receives my formal resignation in writing. All the associates are up to speed with our current cases and any of them is more than qualified to step into my position. It's been my pleasure, sir."

After a quick handshake, Patrick had returned to his office, grabbed his personal possessions and walked out without looking back.

He blew out another heavy sigh as he pulled into the parking deck of his apartment building and parked his car. It had been a long day. Now he had a few hours to kill before his dinner plans with Naomi. He needed a hot shower and a quick nap to rejuvenate himself. And then he needed to figure out his next steps.

Thinking about those next steps had him thinking about Naomi again. He had no doubts that he'd find a new job. He understood his friendship with Garrison and his relationship with the Perry family had reached an impasse. He was resolved to not come back from that. What he wasn't ready to accept was losing Naomi. She was very much a part of his future and he wouldn't have it any other way. She moved him in a manner that left him wanting to be a better man. She was encouraging without even trying, and her enthusiasm was infectious. He hadn't yet found the words to give voice to what he was feeling for her, but she had his heart. She had every ounce of it, and he found himself praying that she wanted it as much as he wanted to give it to her.

Chapter 10

Naomi's laugh rang sweetly through the small restaurant. Everyone around them seemed to smile and laugh with her. When she realized the attention she was getting she blushed profusely, her cheeks a delightful shade of red. Patrick reached for her hand, kissing the backs of her fingers.

"So, that was my day," she said. "Tell me about yours." She propped both elbows on the table and cupped her chin in her palms. "How was your day, honey?"

Patrick laughed. "Clearly, not as eventful as yours!"

"No runaway farm animals for you?"

"Not one! Spent most of my day in meetings, and then I left work early."

Questions danced across her face. "You left early?

Aren't you special! Garrison and Nolan must have been playing hooky, too. You never leave work early!"

"It was that kind of day."

The smile she gave him was bright and full. "There's something I need to talk to you about," she said, her mood seeming to swing from jovial to serious with the batting of her eyelashes.

Patrick shifted nervously in his seat. "Is something wrong?" he asked curiously.

Naomi shook her head. "No… Yes… Well, I have to leave at the end of the week. I need to head back home for a bit."

Patrick nodded. "How long do you think you'll be gone?"

She took in a deep breath, seeming to ponder the question before she answered. "I'm thinking I'll need to be there at least two weeks before I can return to Utah. Maybe three. And that's banking on everything going well. Things here are in a good space and I need to handle some issues at the co-op, so it just makes sense."

His eyes were locked with hers as she continued, "I know you and I are still feeling this relationship out and I hate that I have to go, but I don't have a choice. But we can talk every day and I do plan on coming back."

Patrick drew a breath in turn. "How would you feel if I came along?"

"With me? To Phoenix?"

"Yeah. I would love to join you."

"But you have work?"

"I have some vacation time stored up," he said, the little white lie catching in his chest. He coughed lightly, then cleared his throat. "Work won't be a problem and I would really love to see what your life is like in Arizona. Plus, I've never been there before. I hear Phoenix is a pretty cool city."

Naomi's grin widened. "I think I'd like that. In fact, I like the idea a lot."

"Then we're a go. Let me know your travel plans and I'll book my ticket."

She laughed warmly. "Just pack a bag and be ready when I pick you up on Friday morning. Our travel plans are already handled."

He looked at her curiously and she blessed him with another bright smile.

"My family has its own plane!"

Patrick counted fifteen private planes parked on the tarmac at the general aviation facilities on the east side of the Salt Lake City International Airport. Fifteen planes, two helicopters and a fuel truck.

The day was promising to be a good one, the sun sitting pristinely in a sky that was a deep shade of Carolina blue with the barest spattering of clouds. There was every indication that the weather would be ideal for traveling. Patrick felt himself smiling as he reflected on his decision to invite himself along.

The plane they would be traveling in was being refueled. The flight staff had greeted them both warmly, then had apologized for what would be a longer than anticipated wait to depart. Something to do with a problem on the runway.

The Cessna Citation CJ4 was owned by Naomi's

sister-in-law, her brother Noah's wife. Fly High Dot Com, a private leasing company, was renowned in the industry and the power couple was highly respected. Access to the private carrier was a perk Naomi didn't take lightly. She was on the phone with her brother, expressing her gratitude, as Patrick stared out the floor-to-ceiling windows of the departure area.

"We'll be fine," she was saying as she tossed him her signature smile. "And thank you again, Noah. This really means a lot to me."

She paused, listening intently. Patrick reached for her hand, entwining her fingers with his own as he kissed the back of it. She trailed the pad of her thumb along his jaw.

"I'll tell Patrick what you said," she promised, laughing warmly. "Kiss Cat for me, big brother...I love you, too!"

Patrick smiled as she slid her phone back into her purse. "My brother said to tell you to have a good time."

"That was nice of him."

"He also said to tell you that if you do anything to hurt me, he and the others will track you down and demolish you."

Patrick laughed. "Did he really say that?"

Naomi nodded. "The language was a little rougher, but you get the point," she answered, laughing with him.

He squeezed her fingers. "The next time you talk to him, tell him not to worry."

"I'll do that," she said, as she leaned to kiss his lips.

The gentle touch was just teasing enough to trigger a jolt of energy through his groin. He shifted in his seat, trying to hide the telltale sign threatening to rise to attention. His face flushed with color.

"Are you nervous?" Naomi eyed him curiously.

Shaking his head, he said, "Not at all."

"You look…uncomfortable."

"No, I'm good. Just thinking I should find the men's room before we board."

Naomi pointed over her shoulder. "Down the hall to your left."

Rising, Patrick leaned to give her a quick peck on the cheek. "I'll be right back," he said as he eased past her and sauntered quickly toward where she'd pointed.

Naomi watched as Patrick disappeared down the corridor. His rear view was quite the sight, his denim jeans fitting him nicely through the hips and backside. He had a picture-perfect derriere. He had a cool, buoyant stride, confidence pulling him upright, and she couldn't help but think just how lucky she was, like she'd won the biggest prize at the state fair. He was truly something special and he had a way of making her feel like the most important person in his entire world.

She was excited to have him join her. She wanted Patrick to know everything about her. To experience her life and what she loved most about it. Despite the business that called for her attention, she planned to ensure that the time they spent together was about them and their getting to know each other. If she had her way, it was going to be one quality moment after another.

She looked up as he returned, with a tall brunette chatting eagerly beside him. The woman was giggling as if he'd said something funny. A feeling that felt much like jealousy wafted through the pit of Naomi's stomach. She inhaled swiftly, fighting to keep the emotion from showing on her face.

Patrick suddenly caught her eye and smiled at her. The woman followed his gaze, her expression tightening into the slightest frown. Looking from one to the other, she forced a smile back to her face, something like dismay seeming to fill her dark eyes. Naomi smiled and waved. Patrick grinned broadly, then politely excused himself and moved back to her side. He leaned to kiss her again, his lips meeting hers eagerly.

"That woman tried to pick me up."

Naomi giggled. "That sounds like a personal problem to me."

"You're not jealous?"

"Why should I be? You're with me. It doesn't get any better than that."

Patrick laughed. "You were jealous!"

"I was not."

"Yes, you were. I saw it on your face."

"Please," she said, her eyes skipping around the room.

"It's all good," Patrick replied, as he dropped down into his seat. "I'm jealous when I see other guys looking at you."

"What other guys?"

"Every time we go someplace there's some guy checking out your ass...sets."

Naomi laughed again. "You are so full of it."

He gestured with his head. "Like that old boy over

there. Watch him. Every time he looks at you he licks his lips."

Naomi turned to look, her gaze meeting that of an elderly man who'd been reading. He smiled, his toothy grin reminding her of a beaver. She smiled back and then he dropped his gaze to his magazine again.

She shook her head, glancing at Patrick. "Now you've got jokes."

"I am very serious."

"You're just trying to divert attention from the fact you were flirting with that woman."

"I don't flirt."

"Yes, you do. You're very good at it, actually."

"I'll stop."

"Or just don't do it so well from now on!"

They were both laughing heartily when the flight attendant suddenly appeared before them. "We're ready to board whenever you're ready, Ms. Stallion."

"Thank you." Naomi stood up. She turned to Patrick. "Are you ready, Mr. O'Brien? For the adventure of a lifetime?" she asked, extending her hand.

Patrick's eyes connected with hers, their gazes dancing in perfect sync. He reached out, sliding his palm against hers as he rose to his feet. "I wouldn't miss this time with you for anything in the world," he answered.

Just a few short hours later, Naomi and Patrick arrived in Phoenix. Their energy was infectious, the duo moving strangers to laugh with them as they made their way from the airport to Stallion Farms and Food Co-op.

One of the farmhands, a young man named Miguel,

had arrived in a company truck to pick them up. The teenager chattered away, visibly excited to see Naomi again.

"And then the teacher said that I had the best essay of the whole class and she was submitting it for this contest. Mama was very proud!" His smile was a mile wide as he tossed Naomi and then Patrick a look.

"I'm sure she was, Miguel. I'm very proud of you, too. I told you that you could do it."

He nodded eagerly. "Thank you, Senorita Naomi. I am grateful that you were able to convince the family to stay so that I could finish the school year."

Naomi turned to look at Patrick, who was in the backseat. "Miguel's family is from Mexico. His parents go wherever there's work to support their family. He has a little sister here and two others still in Guadalajara with their grandparents."

"And he's able to go to school here? That's really good."

"Senorita Naomi built a school for us kids on her farm. She says education is very important for us to be successful."

"The senorita is correct," Patrick said, as he tossed Naomi a look.

She shrugged. "Most of the farm workers are migrant and undocumented. They're good people trying to attain a better way of life for their families. I try to offer as much stability for them as I can, and school for the kids helps. We're a registered homeschool program and I employ two teachers year-round. Miguel has been one of our prize pupils. He wants to be a journalist and he's a talented writer."

Miguel pulled in front of the homestead and shifted the vehicle into Park. He left the engine idling. "Senora Morgan says the house is ready. She will be back later this afternoon. One of the new kids has a rash and she took him to see the doctor."

"Thank you, Miguel," Naomi responded. "We'll be down to the fields after we change."

"It was nice to meet you, Senor O'Brien."

"It was nice to meet you, too, Miguel, but please, call me Patrick."

As the youth drove off, waving enthusiastically, Patrick chuckled. "I think Miguel is a little smitten with you."

Naomi laughed. "He's very sweet, but he has a crush on Jamie. She's one of our teachers. He's like a little puppy when she's around. She helped him get a driver's license last year and he's been ecstatic ever since."

"How old is he?"

"Nineteen this year. He finally qualifies for graduation and we're hoping to get him into college in the fall."

"Why would that be a problem?"

Naomi tried to mask her frustration. "His father expects him to work the fields to help support the family."

As Patrick nodded in understanding, Naomi bounded up the steps of the clapboard farmhouse. Grabbing the luggage, he followed. Reaching the porch, he paused, dropping their bags as he leaned against the railing to stare out over the land.

Located just outside the city limits, the farm was

rustic, boasting impressive acreage and vegetation as far as his eyes could see. There was an extraordinary peach orchard, lush green lawns, grapevine-entwined gazebos and large shade trees.

"This is very nice, Naomi."

She turned to look where he stared, pausing for a moment to take it all in herself. She drew a deep breath, swelling with pride. "Thank you. I've actually missed it."

He moved to wrap her in a warm embrace, hugging her tightly. He kissed her, claiming her mouth eagerly. They stood clinging to each other, savoring the sweetness of the moment. Time stood still, allowing them a minute that belonged only to the two of them.

"Let me show you around," Naomi finally said, reluctantly pulling herself out of his arms. She gave him a quick peck on the lips. "Then we have to go to work."

Patrick woke with a start. It took a moment for him to remember where he was and why. At the other end of the oversize sofa Naomi was snoring softly, one arm thrown over her forehead, the other lost somewhere beneath the baggy T-shirt she wore. He sat upright, shifting his body back against the cushions. He eased his leg out from beneath her, mindful not to disturb her rest.

Naomi hadn't been kidding when she said she was putting him to work. After a quick tour of the house, pointing out the bathroom, the kitchen and the guest bedroom, she'd taken him down to the market area, where a team of volunteers and employees were pre-

paring the monthly co-op boxes. He'd lost count of all
the people she'd introduced him to, the names and faces
quickly becoming a blur.

After a quick explanation of how and what, he'd
found himself carting crates of vegetables and fruit
from point A to point B, watching as others dropped
the produce into 279 boxes. Once the boxes were completed, co-op members showed up in droves to pick up
their merchandise.

After the first hour, he'd lost sight of Naomi, who
kept blowing in and out like the sweetest breeze. By
the second hour he'd stopped looking for her, sensing
her presence whenever she was near. A few times she
brushed past him, allowing her body to lightly graze
his as she moved past him. Each time, she blessed him
with a smile, once winking her eye.

When they were finally done it had been pitch-black
out, the sun having disappeared hours earlier. Both were
exhausted, covered in sweat and hungry. Back at the
house Naomi had pulled together a quick salad for two
while he showered and changed. After the light meal,
he'd washed and dried the dishes while she took her
own shower. After a brief conversation about the dry
weather, the benefits of essential oils and his impres-
sions about his first day, they'd fallen asleep on the sofa,
the calming sounds of indigenous music playing from
an iPod speaker in the background. That had been three
days ago, and each day since had gone much the same:
up at dawn, work, then passing out from exhaustion
when it was all over.

Patrick shifted again, moving onto his feet and

heading to the bathroom. After relieving himself, he went back to the main living space and took in his surroundings.

Everything about Naomi's home reflected her carefree personality. The styling was a mix of shabby chic with bright colors and vintage furniture. There were tapestries mixed with linens, chenille spreads on the beds, pillows made of bark-cloth fabric and antique chandeliers hanging from the ceilings. The room was soft and opulent, with a cottage-style vibe. Despite the eclectic layout, it all meshed beautifully together.

He stopped to admire the family photos that lined a mahogany chest. There was the same formal image that had been in her brother's home, plus other pictures of her and her sister, her brothers, and on the wall, a large portrait of her mother. The kitchen boasted Spanish tiles, copper-bottomed pots, an herb garden beneath the window and more of the potted green plants that decorated every room. It was all things Naomi, and standing in the midst of it, Patrick felt more at home than he had in ages.

Still slumbering peacefully, Naomi had stretched her body along the length of the sofa, wrapping herself comfortably around the pillows. She'd tucked her head beneath the lightweight blanket they'd shared earlier, the covering muffling her light snores. Everything about the stunning woman moved his spirit. Her energy was infectious, a glowing light that radiated from her core and embraced everyone around her.

Patrick hadn't known what to expect, nor had he expected to feel so invested in Naomi and their relationship. But he was invested, feeling like he was waging a lifetime out of their short history together. He knew he still needed to tell her he was unemployed, but realized that the life he'd once seen for himself, a life without Naomi, was no longer what he desired. He suddenly realized they needed to sit down and have a serious conversation about what would come next. Because he was determined they should have a future together.

Patrick didn't know how long he'd been standing there, staring at her, watching and wondering what she might be dreaming about. Naomi stirring and throwing her arm back over her head drew him from the reverie he'd fallen into. He took a deep breath, holding the warm air in his lungs as he glanced to the window, to find the hint of sunrise promising another hot day. It wouldn't be long before they'd have to be up. He was still getting accustomed to the intense schedule she thrived on.

He leaned over her, gently pressing a damp kiss against her forehead. He picked up the blanket that had fallen to the floor and tucked it around her torso. Doing an about-face, he sauntered into the guest bedroom and threw himself across the full-size bed. As he closed his eyes, sleep returning, he whispered her name, the beauty of it like spun sugar melting on his tongue.

Chapter 11

Naomi waved for Patrick's attention. He'd been working with Miguel, trying to get the engine in one of the old trucks running. She watched as he acknowledged her with a wave of his own, holding up an index finger. With a nod and a smile, she let him know not to hurry, to come when he was able. She turned back to the wooden plank and the hammer she was using to repair the side of the chicken coop.

She glanced toward him again, watching as he explained something to Miguel. When the roar of the engine suddenly vibrated through the afternoon air, both men whooped with excitement. She laughed at their levity, their exuberance fueling her own.

Patrick had stepped up to help her in ways she couldn't have begun to imagine. It had been two weeks since they'd gotten here and from day one he'd been going full tilt on her behalf. She'd been impressed with how he readily got his hands dirty, finding things that needed to be done before she could even think about them. In the past five days the barn had gotten a new subfloor and her woodpile had been stacked and corded. Freon had been added to the cooling unit in the schoolhouse, he'd helped with the monthly co-op orders and had found time to play a game of soccer with the kids. He'd also adapted to her diet and had proclaimed his energy levels were at a whole new high.

During the few minutes of downtime they'd managed to steal, he asked questions about her business, reviewed her contracts, negotiated a better deal with one of her vendors, all while continually making her laugh. His jokes and one-line zingers continually kept a smile on her face and Naomi couldn't remember when she'd been so happy.

Their friendship had grown exponentially. There was nothing they didn't feel comfortable talking about. Everything from politics to her menstrual cycle to his favorite Saturday morning cartoons had been the topic of discussion at one time or another. He continued to be overly affectionate and playful, and seemed intent on insuring she was at the forefront of every action he took. He had her feeling immensely loved despite neither one of them having ventured to be the first to express what they were feeling out loud. And admittedly, what Naomi was feeling for Patrick was deeply intense. She had allowed herself to be vulnerable, opening herself to him in a way that was completely foreign to her. He had yet to disappoint her, and she trusted him. And Naomi didn't trust any man. Patrick had her feeling as if she'd stepped into an emotional fire and was surviving the flames unscathed.

Thinking about him, she suddenly recalled a pre-dawn encounter earlier that week that had left them both panting with anticipation. A bad dream had pulled her from a deep sleep. She'd been lying half on, half off the living room sofa, a spot she and Patrick frequently found themselves in since he'd settled into her home. She'd risen, believing he had moved to the guest room bed, where the early-morning sun often found him.

Heading to her own bedroom, she'd stripped out of the clothes she'd fallen asleep in, changing to an over-size dress shirt that she didn't bother to button. Feeling thirsty, she went back to the kitchen for a glass of water. She was surprised to find Patrick standing in front of the refrigerator, guzzling the last of the freshly squeezed orange juice from the plastic container. He stood bare-chested, wearing only a pair of bright white boxer briefs that outlined his curves and bulges. The sliver of moonlight shining through the kitchen win-dow was like a spotlight on his chiseled muscles and café au lait complexion. He was beautiful!

Her very audible gasp startled him, and he turned abruptly to find her staring at him.

"I'm sorry, did I wake you?" Patrick asked, his own eyes widening. His gaze was focused on the bare flesh peeking past her opened shirt, the round of her breasts and the slightly protruding belly button that drew his eye to the lace panties that barely covered her feminine quadrant. He blinked rapidly as he forced himself to shift his eyes upward to her face.

Naomi had shaken her head. "No, I just needed a glass of water. Are you okay?"

Patrick smiled, his arm and the empty juice bottle dropping to conceal the rise of nature that was suddenly swelling in his briefs. He turned toward the counter and set the container in the sink. He nodded, his voice cracking. "I think I'm good."

Naomi laughed. She moved behind him, reaching into the cabinet for a glass. He was still clutching the edge of the sink as he waited for her to fill it from the refrigerator door, then slowly drink the water down. When she was done, she passed behind him a second time, setting the glass in the sink beside the juice jug. Then she pressed her palm to his back, her fingers gliding over his flesh. Her touch moved him to inhale swiftly.

"Are you sure you're okay?"

"You're killing me, Naomi. You know that, right?" The aroused look he gave her was all telling.

She laughed, the sound echoing through the late-night air. He suddenly turned, gliding an arm beneath her shirt and around her waist as he pulled her tightly against him. His touch was electric and she inhaled swiftly. Bare skin kissed bare skin as he dropped his mouth to hers and claimed her lips in a tongue-entwined kiss. Naomi wasn't sure how long he held her, time seeming to come to a standstill as they reveled in being so close to each other.

And then the phone rang, the loud peal surprising

them both. They turned to stare at the device that hung on the kitchen wall, as if it was a throwback to another time and place. Neither one of them made any effort to answer it.

"Why do you still have a house phone?" Patrick asked.

Naomi shrugged. "It comes in handy when someone needs to call home to Mexico. And the international calls are cheaper than on my cell phone."

The ringing suddenly stopped, and they both listened for a voice message to be left on the recorder in her bedroom. There was a moment's pause, then a click, then a dial tone that faded into silence.

Patrick heaved a deep sigh. She was speechless when he leaned in close to her ear and said, "I want you, and right now I'm thinking about how many ways I can have you in this kitchen. But I need to know it's what you want and that you want it as much as I do."

The phone suddenly rang a second time. He shook his head. "Answer the phone," he said, then pressed a kiss to her cheek and stepped back. "We'll finish this conversation later."

That night, he'd gone back to the spare bedroom while Naomi put out a fire with one of her workers, an illness across the border calling someone home. She and Patrick still hadn't finished their conversation, "later" having yet to happen. Naomi needed to tell him that she wanted him as much as he wanted her, if not more.

She shifted her attention back to Patrick now and watched as he and the teen gave each other a high five. He slammed down the hood of the truck, then wiped his hands with an old rag that he tucked into the back pocket of his jeans. As Miguel jumped into the vehicle and drove off across the farmyard, Patrick sauntered toward her.

"Sorry about that," he said as he moved close, leaning to kiss her cheek. "Do you need help with something?"

Naomi shook her head. "No. I'm done here and I was thinking that we should go have ourselves a picnic lunch. Unless there's something else you want to do?"

"You mean you're actually going to let me take a break?"

Naomi laughed. "You say that like I'm working you to death or something!"

"Well, if the tractor fits..." His smile widened, filling his face with immeasurable joy.

"Oh, no, you don't! Like the Perrys never had you working 24/7?"

"Pushing papers is one thing. Pushing farm equipment is a whole other beast."

"It'll keep you fit."

He kissed her again. "Glad to hear you're concerned about my body."

She eased her hands around his waist, clutching the T-shirt he wore. "Someone needs to be concerned. Otherwise, you'd be soft and flabby by the time you're fifty, and that would not be a good look, Counselor."

For a quick moment, he pondered her comment, Naomi calling him "counselor" nipped at a nerve. Then he smiled. "I would love to have lunch with you," he said, as he gently trailed his thumb against her cheek. "And a picnic sounds perfect."

Naomi grinned. "Great! Go grab a shower and let's have some fun!"

The drive to Scottsdale and their picnic at the mall took no time at all. Patrick enjoyed being able to just sit back and take it all in. It was a beautiful day, sun filled, cloudless, with just enough breeze to keep the heat at bay. Naomi chattered easily beside him, as excited for them to spend time alone as he was.

He reached across the center console and drew his hand along her arm. His gentle touch was warm and heated, and sent a shiver along the length of Naomi's spine. She giggled softly.

"You need to stop," she said, her voice low and hushed.

"Stop what?" He continued to caress her, his fingers moving to the back of her neck, then twirling a strand of her hair around his finger.

Her body quivered and she shook her shoulders. "That," she said, shooting him a sly smile. "What you're doing with your hands."

He continued to tease her skin, gently kneading her shoulders. "I'm sorry. Is this bothering you?" The pad of his index finger swirled in tiny circles across her forearm.

She laughed. "It's… We… You know what it's doing to me!"

Patrick shifted in his seat, continuing to tease her. "No, tell me," he said.

Not bothering to answer, she reached for the radio instead and turned on the sound system, flooding the vehicle with an energetic pop song.

Patrick chuckled. "So now you're not talking to me?"

"I'm talking."

"So, tell me what my touching you is doing to you."

Naomi shot him another look, her eyes narrowed slightly. A few minutes passed before she finally answered. "You're not funny, Patrick O'Brien. You know you excite me. You know that when you touch me, I want you to keep touching me. So I don't know why you're teasing me!"

A gargantuan grin exploded across his face as he leaned closer. "How much do you like it?" He dropped his hand and trailed his fingers over her thigh, in one direction and back again.

Naomi tensed, heat rising with a vengeance. Her eyes skated from the roadway, to her rearview and side mirrors and then to him. "You are so not funny! Keep that up and you're going to make me wreck this car."

Patrick held up his palms as if surrendering and laughed heartily. "You are so cute right now! Look at you!"

Naomi laughed with him. "When I can put my hands on you, I am so going to hurt you!"

"Promise?"

"Why are you giving me such a hard time right now?"

"Because I want to make love to you," he said matter-of-factly. He was staring at her intently, the intoxicating look moving her to smile and her face to flush with color.

He continued, "It's getting harder and harder for me to hide how much I want us to be together, Naomi. I don't want you to feel rushed or pressured, but I'm not going to hide it any longer. I want you."

She took a deep breath, again, and then another. "Can we change the subject and talk about this later? When I'm not driving. Please?"

"Do you ever think about making love to me, Naomi?"

"Patrick, can we—"

"Because I think about it all the time. I go to sleep at night dreaming about being inside you. I wake up in the morning thinking about how incredible it would be to start my day with you riding me. I spend half my day with a raging hard-on because I can't stop thinking about you. So, do you ever imagine what it would be like to be with me? Do you want that?"

Naomi shot him a look. "Patrick, I think about it all the time, too. Because I do want to make love to you! I am so ready for us to take that next step that I can't tell you how much I want it to happen." She swung her gaze his way, meeting his stare. "Now, can we please change the subject so I can focus on getting us to our destination safely?"

He whooped loudly, making them both laugh. "I just needed to check," he said with a wink. "Because you had me feeling a little insecure."

"I did not!"

His head moved up and down. "You really did. I

was starting to wonder if maybe I was losing my touch. Woman, you know how fragile the male ego is! You have definitely had mine on edge."

She laughed again. "You're usually very intuitive, Mr. O'Brien. I was sure you knew how I was feeling."

"A man still needs to ask. But you focus on the road. We can finish this conversation later."

Naomi felt the heat that rushed to color her cheeks, imagining that she was probably bright red. "We most certainly will," she said.

The Scottsdale Mall wasn't what Patrick had been expecting. Instead, the public space was a park with an exquisite greenway of lush lawns and floral gardens adorned with fountains and a multitude of art. The surrounding area boasted an old tavern, an Iron Chef–owned bistro, a public library and the Scottsdale Museum of Contemporary Art. It was the perfect midday getaway.

Naomi had packed them a Southwestern salad of mixed baby greens topped with black beans, sweet corn and grape tomatoes drizzled with a tangy avocado-lime dressing. For dessert, there was fresh mixed berries— strawberries, raspberries, blackberries and blueberries. It was a light, nourishing meal and, with her homemade ginger beer, a delightful treat.

They talked about everything and nothing. Neither bothered to speak about the sexual attraction that had become a consistent force of nature between them, nor bring up the subject of taking their relationship to the next level. That conversation was over, both of them understanding that the next step would come easily, a natural progression of where they inevitably saw themselves. Excitement simmered just under the skin, the two intoxicated by the prospect of what lay ahead for them, no words necessary to explain it.

The ride back to Phoenix and the farm was quiet. Both fell into their own thoughts about each other, what had brought them together and what was keeping them connected. There was an ease about being together that filled them both with joy. Even the silence they shared spoke volumes.

Naomi pulled onto the dirt road that led toward the house. As she parked the car and shut down the engine, Patrick shifted in his seat, turning to face her.

He cleared his throat. "Naomi, there's something I need to tell you. I haven't been totally honest with you."

They locked gazes, Naomi suddenly feeling a wave of nervous tension punch her in the gut.

"I swear, Patrick, if you tell me you're married, I will dump you into the feed grinder and fertilize the fields with you."

He chuckled. "I am not married. I have never been married. And when I do marry I imagine you'll be right there by my side."

She gave him a nod and a slight smile. "So, what is it? Because you're suddenly scaring me."

"I wasn't altogether honest with you about my job. I didn't have any vacation time saved up."

Confusion washed over Naomi's face. "I don't understand. Did you take a leave of absence or something?"

"I'm no longer employed by the Perry Group. We mutually agreed to end our business relationship."

Naomi's eyes flickered back and forth as she took in the news. She suddenly gasped. "Oh, my God! Nolan fired you! Nolan fired you because of me."

Patrick reached for her hands, pulling them between his own. "No. I quit, because I had no respect for how he was treating you. Because I couldn't be the man you deserved if I had continued to work for them, knowing they were wrong."

He took a deep inhalation and then explained, going back to his last days in the office and everything that had happened. When he was finished, a tear had fallen against Naomi's cheek. She swiped it away with the back of her hand.

"You really should have told me," she said, her voice dropping an octave.

"I'm telling you now. I didn't tell you before because I didn't want you agonizing over it, and I knew you well enough to know that it would have been a wedge between us."

"It's a wedge now. That was your job. Your *j-o-b*! I never would have asked you to quit your job for me. Do you know how hard it is these days for some people to get work?"

"Naomi, I quit because I didn't want to be affiliated with any organization that thinks it's okay to attack people they believe are in their way. I could never align myself with Garrison or his father and feel good about myself. Them going after you was the final straw."

Naomi shook her head. She pulled her hands from

his and exited the car. The sky had begun to darken, the last sliver of sunlight disappearing over the horizon. Walking slowly across the grassy knoll, she wrapped her arms around her torso and hugged herself tightly. Even with all the miles and distance between them, Nolan Perry had managed to once again touch her small world and inflict pain. And not only had he hurt her, but he'd again hurt someone she cared about. There was no stopping the hot tears that rained down her cheeks.

When Patrick eased up behind her, wrapping his arms around her and pulling her tightly against him, she was sobbing. They stood beneath the bright light of a full moon as he let her cry until she was all cried out.

She finally heaved a deep sigh. "You really shouldn't have quit," she voiced softly. "You loved that job."

He stood in reflection for a moment, then gave her a light squeeze. Shifting even closer, he leaned his forehead against her hair and tightened his grasp. "No. What I love is you. I love you, Naomi. You have captured my whole heart. I can't begin to imagine what my life would be like without you. I love you so much, it scares the hell out of me and excites me at the same time. So there was no way I could have continued to work for the Perry family."

He heard her gasp softly, her body beginning to quiver again in his arms. He spun her around, chuckling softly. "You're not supposed to cry when a man tells you he loves you, baby. You're really beginning to give me a complex."

She laughed, wrapping herself around him as she pressed her face to his chest. She hugged him tightly.

Overwhelmed with emotion, she batted her thick lashes to stall the saline that misted her gaze.

Patrick cupped his hand beneath her chin and lifted her face. "I love you. And I'm not going to let anything or anyone come between us. Not now. Not ever." He leaned and kissed her lips, the gentle touch cementing the promise.

Naomi's tears fell for a second time. She hadn't allowed herself to define what she was feeling for Patrick. It had been easy to just let what was building between them take on a life of its own. They'd found a level of comfort with each other that had needed no words, and she, too, couldn't begin to think about not having that in her life. He meant the world to her, and after fighting her initial reservations, she had no intention of losing him without one hell of a fight.

She threw her arms around his neck and kissed him again, her mouth skating easily against his. The kiss lasted until both needed to come up for air. "I love you, too, Patrick! I love you so much. I never thought I'd love anyone as much as I love you," she gushed. "But I'm still really pissed about you quitting your job!"

Patrick laughed as he kissed her one more time. Her words were music to his ears, the sweetest symphony.

Chapter 12

Patrick had swept Naomi off her feet. Literally. Sweeping her up and into his arms, he'd carried her up the front steps and over the threshold into the small home. Inside, he hadn't wanted to let her go, determined to hold her close for as long as he was able.

In the middle of the living room, they'd stood together trading easy caresses and the gentlest kisses. When he finally released his hold on her it was only to move them both to the sofa. As Naomi eased herself back against the pillows, Patrick dropped down beside her. She wrapped her arms and legs around him, pulling him close as his mouth reclaimed hers.

Patrick slid his hand to the back of her neck and she moaned, a jolt of electricity passing between them and settling nicely in the pit of their midsections. Naomi felt her panties dampen, moisture puddling between her legs. He slid his tongue across her upper lip, then back across her lower one. It was rough and bold and urgent, and he tasted sweet, like hot honey. He slipped his tongue past the line of her teeth, meeting hers like he was greeting an old friend. As they touched, both moaned into each other's mouth, tongues dueling and dancing. When their mouths finally parted, he pressed his forehead to hers, both of them struggling to catch their breath.

There was something magical about the way Patrick touched her. He caressed her face with his fingertips, gently gliding over her earlobes and down the length of her neck, the journey slow and sensuous. His feathery touch tickled her skin, his ministrations heated. He eased an arm around her torso as he slipped his other hand beneath her shirt and gently teased one breast and then the other. He used his thumb and forefinger to twist and pinch her nipples, which blossomed full and hard, rock candy that she hoped had Patrick salivating for a taste of.

Naomi gasped, her breath catching somewhere deep in her chest as she purred with pleasure. She suddenly grabbed his wrist, stalling his ministrations. His eyes widened as she pushed him gently away and eased her body from his. She extended her hand, something decadent and sensual oozing from her eyes. Patrick took the hand she offered and followed as she led him to the master bedroom.

He stood watching as Naomi pulled her blouse up and over her head. She slowly undid the zipper to her cotton slacks and pushed them down to her feet. Beneath her clothes she wore royal blue satin, her push-up bra and panties trimmed in eyelet lace. She was stunning, the sexy lingerie flattering her figure nicely. His eyes widened as she reached around for the clasp, and as she undid it, she turned, moving into the bathroom.

He chuckled softly as he followed like an eager puppy. When he reached the door Naomi was stepping into the shower, blue satin discarded on the bathroom floor. Her naked form took his breath away, every square inch of bare flesh calling for his attention. His male member hardened with a vengeance, the rod of steel pulling so tight it felt as if the seam of his jeans would burst from the strain.

Naomi turned to face him, trailing a soapy palm between her breasts down to the taut muscles of her abdomen. Her pubic hair curled tightly and she let her fingers tease the triangular patch, drawing his gaze as he stood watching. She gestured with her other hand, a crooked index finger beckoning him to her. There was something intoxicating about the look she was giving him, a sparkle of mischief in the warmth of her stare. She arched her eyebrows and gave him a smile that sent his temperature skyrocketing.

Patrick suddenly realized he'd been holding his breath. He gulped, sucking in air, and then he was out of his clothes before she could blink. Both laughed nervously as he stepped into the shower, reaching for her as his eagerness stirred between his legs for her attention. He actually cried out, a little scream that evolved to a long, low groan, as he wrapped his arms around

Naomi and she wrapped her fingers around his erection. Every nerve ending pulsed and twitched beneath her grasp, the appendage throbbing in sync with his heartbeat and hers. It was pleasure like he'd never experienced before as she stroked him gently.

The water running from the showerhead was warm, the room beginning to steam nicely with heat. It swirled around them, finding its way into every nook and cranny. Naomi felt as if she'd been exported to another time and place, she and Patrick performing an exotic dance of give-and-take as they discovered every intimate detail about each other.

He suddenly dropped to his knees, gently guiding one leg over his shoulder. When he pressed his mouth to her sweet spot, Naomi thought she might fall to the floor in ecstasy. The sensations he was eliciting with his tongue as he lapped at her nectar had her quivering, her muscles weak, every nerve ending snapping to attention. He licked every inch of her, lightly at first, flicking at her clit, then probing deeper. She wiggled and twisted, moving her hips in a slow, seductive motion, moving with him as he savored the taste of her.

Naomi hissed out a low gust of air. "Yes!" She pressed a palm to the back of his head and clutched the shower rail with her other hand to steady herself.

When her orgasm hit, it erupted with a ferocity Naomi didn't expect. She screamed his name, clutching his head as she pushed herself against his tongue. Her body quaked, the intensity unlike anything she could describe. He kept licking as wave after wave of indescribable euphoria cascaded through her and she collapsed against the tiled wall, water still washing down over them both.

For the second time that day Patrick swept her up into his arms. He carried her from the shower to the bed, dragging the covers to the floor before he eased her onto the mattress. In the other room the water was still running and neither cared. Naomi gestured toward the nightstand. "Condoms," she whispered huskily.

Patrick opened the drawer. Inside, a brand-new, un-opened box of prophylactics rested in a corner. Naomi lay sprawled across the dampened sheets, panting softly. He smiled as he tore at the cellophane, claimed one from inside and quickly sheathed himself. As he crawled above her, Naomi pulled him in, her mouth and body meeting his. He kissed her fervently, his tongue searching as he pushed her legs open, spreading her wide. He teased her, grinding his pelvis against hers, back and forth, over and over again.

"Don't tease me," she gasped.

"You want this?" he whispered back, still crushing his body against hers, the slow gyrations moving her to moan softly.

"You know I do."

"Say it!"

Naomi's breathing was labored, coming in quick gasps as her body twitched with anticipation. "I want you, Patrick!"

"Say it again!"

"I want…want… I want you… Patrick, I want…" She stammered, words failing her as she reveled in the sensation of his touch.

Patrick suddenly pushed her legs forward. He hooked his arms behind her knees and then he entered her, sliding his length into her in one swift motion. Naomi gasped, surprised by the fullness that suddenly possessed her body. Patrick began to work his hips back and forth, slowly sliding in and out of her. Heat began to build as her body rose from the mattress to meet him stroke for stroke. She gasped again, then murmured his name, chanting it over and over like a favored mantra.

His strokes were slow and easy, then fast and furious, in and out, out and in. With each push and pull she tightened around him, squeezing him harder and harder. The friction of his body inside hers pushed them both to the edge of an abyss and then dropped them over the side. Naomi orgasmed a second time, and when she did, Patrick came with her. Every muscle tensed with unadulterated desire as he pushed himself into her and screamed her name, before collapsing above her. They both cried out, their voices ringing with glee as they shuddered and trembled together, riding the wave of each orgasmic aftershock. The intensity of the moment was more than either could have ever imagined.

When Naomi opened her eyes, sunlight was coming through the windows of her bedroom. She rolled toward the edge of the bed to steal a quick glance at the alarm clock resting on the nightstand. It was well past ten in the morning, the alarm having sounded hours earlier. Beside her, Patrick was still sleeping, low snores vibrating past his lips. Watching him brought a smile to her face as she remembered the lovemaking that had lasted into the early-morning hours. She had lost count of the number of times he had brought her to orgasm, each cataclysmic outburst more powerful than the last. She imagined the dull ache between her legs would be a pleasant reminder through the day of all they had shared.

She reached for her cell phone and sent a text message to her staff. She didn't want them looking for her when she had no intention of leaving the house. It wasn't often that she allowed herself to play hooky from work, but she had plans for her and Patrick that had nothing to do with the business or the farm. Dropping the device back to the nightstand, she eased herself out of bed and into the bathroom. After a quick wash and dry, she headed into the kitchen, suddenly famished.

It was the sound of an electric appliance that eventually pulled Patrick from slumber. He reached an arm out, and when he found the bed empty, he opened his eyes. Despite feeling energized, his body was still fatigued, but in a pleasant way. He had no complaints as he thought about the previous night, the memories flooding his mind. A wide grin creased his face as he palmed the morning erection suddenly throbbing for attention. He rose and walked naked into the bathroom to relieve himself. After brushing his teeth and washing his face, he went in search of Naomi.

She was standing at the kitchen counter, cutting fruits and vegetables before passing them through a juicer. Naomi was topless, wearing only a pair of pale pink panties. Her dreadlocks were pulled into a high ponytail, a printed silk scarf wound intricately around her head. She smiled when she saw him staring. "Good morning, sleepyhead!"

"Hey, you! Don't you look delicious this morning."

She giggled. "Thank you. You look quite yummy yourself," she said, as she nodded toward the bulge that hung heavy between his legs.

Patrick laughed as he leaned to kiss her. "So, what are you up to?"

"Making juice for our breakfast. You need to get your energy back up and this will do the trick."

He reached for the glass she extended toward him, his face skewed in a mock snarl.

She continued, "It's good for you. It's beets, carrots, apples and spinach. Now, drink up. And it doesn't taste bad at all, so stop playing."

Amused, Patrick eyed her with a hint of skepticism, not quite convinced.

Naomi laughed. "Drink and then I'll take care of that personal problem you have there," she said, as her eyes dropped low, then lifted back to his face. She licked her lips, the salacious gesture pulling his own smile wider.

"Well, if you insist," he said, then chugged the drink, swallowing it in a few quick gulps.

She laughed again as she sipped her own drink.

"So, what's on our agenda today?" he asked, as he leaned over the countertop. "We're late for work, aren't we?"

She moved to the sink, washing both glasses and the juicer. "The boss gave us the day off," she answered, tossing him a look.

Patrick grinned. "I guess I'll have to show the boss my appreciation," he said, as he moved to her side.

He slid a hand across her buttocks, gently squeezing one cheek and then the other. Naomi giggled again as she turned toward him, pressing her body against his. She raised her mouth and kissed him, finding the taste of apples and toothpaste on their breath. Patrick suddenly lifted her from the floor, setting her atop the counter. He eased one finger under the elastic of her panties. Heat radiated from the gap between her thighs. Her body quivered with anticipation as he gently explored her intimate folds and his thumb tapped at the hood of her clit. Naomi opened herself even further, widening her legs to allow him easier access.

Patrick slid his hand in deeper, teasing the soft curls on her mound. A second finger and then a third and fourth dived between her parted legs. He slid them in and out of her as he coated each with her wetness. Naomi began to rock herself against his knuckles, her head tossed back in pure, unadulterated pleasure.

When Patrick pulled his hand from her, she'd come at least twice, the sensations leaving her dazed. Naomi watched as he moved his fingers to his lips and licked them, one by one, tasting the sweetness of her juices. He hummed in appreciation as he winked at her. She shook her head as she slid back down to the floor.

Naomi moved to the refrigerator, searching until she found a jar of homemade strawberry preserves tucked away in the back. "Would you open this for me?" she asked, passing him the container.

Patrick laughed. "Really, Naomi?" he quipped as he twisted off the cap.

Amusement painted her expression. "A girl is hungry," she said, her expression smug. "Very hungry!"

Laughter danced in his eyes when she pressed a palm to his chest and gently pushed him toward a stool at the counter. Sitting down, he found himself twitching with excitement as she dipped a spoon into the sweet confection and dropped a mound of it directly onto his lap, berries and jelly dripping down his shaft and tangling in his pubic hair. He jumped, his eyes widening, as the appendage hardened in anticipation.

Moving between his legs, Naomi dropped to her knees before him. She planted a trail of damp kisses against his inner thighs, then glided strawberries up and down his member with her tongue. Patrick moaned, a deep guttural utterance that came from someplace deep in his midsection.

She played with him, toying with him, stroking him gently as she licked the sugar from his testicles. She took one into her mouth and then the other. Above her, Patrick moaned, his hips beginning to bounce lightly up and down. Her teasing had him rigid, his yearning so intense he was past ready to explode. Naomi slid her tongue gently along the underside of his shaft, swirling it in small circles, and then her wet mouth enveloped him, her cheeks bulging.

"Oh, yeah," Patrick muttered softly. "Just like that!"

Naomi continued to pleasure him with her mouth. Her tongue, lips and hands moved with near-perfect technique. He was panting heavily, in awe of just how good it all felt. Her tongue danced over the head, down the length, lashing at his scrotum and back again. She licked him like a lollipop, then sucked him as if drinking her favorite beverage through a straw. She lapped at him, over and over, until every ounce of the sweet confection was gone and he was ready to explode.

"Don't make me come," Patrick quipped as he shifted his hips back and away. He pulled himself from her grasp.

Naomi sat back on her haunches, swiping at her lips with her fingers. Standing, Patrick searched out the necessary protection, then returned to pull her to her feet. He kissed her neck, suckling the soft flesh, before moving to one breast and then the other. He nuzzled his face between the soft swells, inhaling the sweetest hint of jasmine that scented her skin.

Pleasure blessed her center—a deep, intoxicating hedonism that woke something inside her core that had been dormant for longer than she realized. She found herself craving it, lusting after it, unable to fathom how she'd not known how much she needed it.

He suddenly spun her around, sheathing himself quickly before bending her forward over the counter. He entered her swiftly, taking her from behind. He pushed himself into her until her buttocks were cradled tightly against his pelvis. Naomi moaned, completely incapable of speech. They were lost in a multitude of sensations as he drove himself in and out of her, harder and harder, slow, then fast.

Their loving moved from one room to the other, leaving no corner of the house left untouched. Morning turned into afternoon as they spent the day exploring and loving each other. In bed and out they ravished one another, savoring orgasm after orgasm until they were too spent to even walk. Then, hand in hand, wrapped warmly around each other, they sat on the screened porch and watched the sun set.

Chapter 13

Naomi and Patrick fell into a comfortable routine with one another. They had returned to Salt Lake City and been back to Phoenix twice more since their first trip. Patrick still hadn't given any thought to finding another job, uncovering much joy in getting his hands dirty on Naomi's farms. Since he'd left the Perry Group, Garrison had called him multiple times, wanting to renew their friendship and go back to the way they had been with each other. But Patrick wasn't interested in anything Garrison had to offer. He wasn't interested in returning to any place where Naomi wasn't welcomed with him. He didn't bother to return his old friend's calls.

The co-op in Salt Lake City was just weeks away from opening. Naomi had invested her heart and soul into replicating the business model that was so successful in Phoenix. Patrick was enjoying being a part of her efforts. Her successes felt as if they were as much his as they were hers.

He stared at her from the window of her home, as she stood outside, gazing out over the land. Clearly, her mind was still racing as she plotted her next steps and planned what she needed to do. They had spent most of the night brainstorming as she ran ideas past him, seeking out his advice. He'd been delighted to give her his thoughts, even though at times he had to admit that he didn't have a clue. He enjoyed learning her business, finding much gratification in the busywork that required more brawn from him than brain. But he recognized that brain was why she was often lauded for her accomplishments. Naomi was smart as a whip, yet never allowed her intelligence to overshadow her good nature.

She challenged him when he least expected it. They both took great pleasure in debating their respective opinions. Naomi could give as good as she took and she never cut him any slack. He was smitten with her gentle approach to life, her compassionate spirit and her love for her fellow man. She motivated him to want to be a better man. Naomi was in a class of her own making and he often wondered what he had done to become so immensely blessed.

His father chuckled softly into the telephone. The two had been talking for a good long while, Patrick updating him on everything that had happened since their last conversation. Both his parents had been supportive of his decision to take a break while he figured out what he wanted to do next with his life. They knew his finances were in order, and he had invested well. His savings would carry him for quite some time, even if he decided never to practice law again. They also knew that for him to be reevaluating his future, something or someone had made a serious impact on his life.

"So, how long will you be in Phoenix this time, Hijo?" his father asked.

"I'm not quite sure. I'm thinking at least one week, if not two."

"When do you think you might get home to Miami? Your mother misses you. And I wouldn't mind seeing you sometime soon myself."

Patrick nodded into the receiver. "Naomi and I were just talking about that. I really want her to meet you and Mama. And, honestly, we could both use a vacation. So I hope very soon."

"Well, keep us posted, Hijo."

"I will, Papi. Give Mama a hug and kiss for me please. And I'll talk to you again soon."

"I love you, Hijo!"

"I love you, too, Papi."

Disconnecting the call, Patrick continued to stare out the kitchen window. Truth be told, he couldn't wait to introduce Naomi to the only other woman who had a claim on his heart. Zora O'Brien and Naomi Stallion were the two most important women in his small world. He couldn't fathom life without either of them.

He moved from the window to the back door and stepped out onto the porch. Naomi turned and waved. Patrick waved back, genuine joy flooding his spirit.

He could feel that it was going to be a very good day. Stealing a quick glance at his wristwatch, he realized they still had a good hour before anyone would be looking for them. One hour to make the sweetest love to the woman he loved with all his heart.

Hours later Patrick was standing in conversation with Miguel's father, the young man listening in as Patrick tried to explain the importance of Miguel pursuing a college education. The older man was adamant that his son follow in his footsteps, migrating from farm to farm to help support the family. Naomi had given it her best shot, but the man wasn't having it. He was of a different generation, believing that good, old-fashioned hard work would best serve them all. He didn't see the need for higher education for his son to become successful. He couldn't see past his own dreams to accept the dreams Miguel had for himself.

Just as the conversation was drawing to an end, Naomi came racing in their direction. Her usual exuberance was dimmed substantially. Patrick had never seen her so anxious, something clearly playing havoc with her spirit. Concern flashed through him as she rushed up to meet him, tears misting her eyes.

"What's wrong, baby?"

"We need to fly back to Utah, immediately. Someone has set fire to the crops at Norris Farms."

He gripped her shoulders to steady her, the severity of the situation hitting home. No wonder she was shivering, anxiety flooding her spirit.

"What happened?"

Naomi shook her head. "No one's sure. Noah just called me. But we've lost the crop. It's all gone."

Patrick hugged her close, wrapping an arm around her back as his other hand tangled in her hair. He kissed the top of her head, feeling her body trembling against him. "You go pack. I'll make sure everything's good here and I'll let everyone know we're leaving."

"We won't be here for this month's co-op pickup." She twisted her hands together anxiously.

"Not to worry, Senorita Naomi," Miguel interjected. "We will make sure that you have no problems."

His father nodded in agreement.

"*Muchas gracias*. I appreciate that," Naomi said with a slight smile. "Thank you." She reached to give the teenager and his father each a hug. Then she walked back into Patrick's arms one last time before heading toward the farmhouse. "I can't believe this is happening," she murmured as he hugged her tightly. "Who would do such a thing?"

The fire at Norris Farms was the lead story with all the local media outlets. When Naomi and Patrick landed, Noah picked them up at the airport and rushed them to the property. The local Fox TV affiliate, WSTU, was parked at the entrance gate. Many others had left messages hoping for exclusive interviews. The police had cordoned off the property and were still investigating. No one had any answers for them.

"I'm ruined," Naomi muttered beneath her breath.

"You are not ruined," Noah responded.

She fought back the tears that threatened to fall past

her dark lashes. Patrick reached out a warm hand and trailed it gently against her back. Naomi lifted her eyes to his, staring intently into them. Everything about the look he was giving her was meant to calm her nerves and give her strength to forge ahead. In that moment, he didn't know that although she was saddened, she was also angry.

Together, the trio walked the expansive property, assessing the damage. Patrick made mental notes to call the insurance company, her vendors, the bank, and to arrange for additional staff to help clear away the ash, revitalize the soil with nitrogen and replant the land as soon as they were able. Neither he nor Naomi was a stranger to hard work and he knew they had much hard work ahead of them.

Marcella cried when they stopped by the homestead to check in, grateful the old farmhouse had not been touched. The woman was beside herself, racked with guilt that she couldn't have done something to stop the vandals who had done the damage.

"It's not your fault," Naomi assured her.

"There's nothing you could have done," Patrick added.

"No one was injured and that's what's most important," Noah interjected.

Days later, as the work of tilling the soil and replanting began, Naomi was still questioning who could have done such a thing. Why had she been targeted? And who could possibly have been that evil to wish to do her harm? She had wanted to believe the blaze had been an accident, but when the local fire department confirmed that arson had been the cause of the flames, she'd been devastated. Now the frustration of not knowing haunted her.

"Let it go," Patrick intoned.

"I can't. I can't let it go until we find out who did it."

"And what if we don't find out?"

"Someone knows something."

Patrick nodded. He knew she was right, but he also knew she was starting to obsess over it, and that was quickly becoming an issue for them.

Days later, when his phone rang, Garrison Perry greeted him from the other end. "You don't call your friends back anymore?"

"What do you want, Garrison?"

"I was wondering how much longer you're going to let this go on. When are you coming back to the fold?"

Patrick hesitated, having no words to respond. He did miss his old friend. He missed the young man he had often joked with, who had moments of compassion for others. The one he had shared secrets with and once called his best friend. He missed that man.

Garrison continued, "So, are you still dating that Stallion woman? You get her out of your system yet?"

The Garrison Patrick didn't miss was suddenly back in full form. A heavy sigh hissed past his lips.

"This really isn't a good time."

"It's never a good time for you these days. I hated to hear about that fire. I'm sure it was a huge loss for your friend."

"Naomi is just fine. But I'm sure she'll appreciate your concern."

"Well, my offer still stands if she's interested in selling. Of course, I'll have to reduce that offer, considering the damage that was done. I'm sure that gasoline couldn't have been good for the soil."

"Who said anything about gasoline?"

There was no hesitation before Garrison responded. "I think my father said something. He read it in the paper somewhere. Or maybe he heard it on the news. I don't remember. But does it matter?"

Patrick paused, listening as the other man ran on, yammering about his latest antics on the dating scene. For a split second, Patrick had found himself smiling, the moment feeling like old times, and then Garrison fell back into his old habits.

"She has a friend. A real hottie with tits and ass for days. I'll introduce you and we can double date. What do you say?"

With nothing left to say, Patrick cut the call short. After disconnecting, he thought back on the conversation. He didn't want to believe it, but there was a nagging thought in the back of his mind that maybe Garrison or Giselle or both had made good on their threats to sabotage Naomi.

Naomi entering the room interrupted his thoughts. She eyed him curiously. "Are you okay? You look like you just lost your best friend."

Patrick shrugged, then shook his head. "My best friend is right here and she's just fine." He leaned over to give her a quick kiss. "So, I'm good. How about you?"

"To be honest, honey, I don't know if I'm coming or going. I know I have a meeting this afternoon with a grain supplier. I hope to plant wheat on that acreage in the back, if we can get a good price for the seed. The rest is just a blur."

"You need to get away. We should think about taking a vacation and maybe head down to Miami."

Naomi's eyes shifted from side to side as she pondered his comment. "I'd like that, but I'm not sure it's a good time for me to get away. Maybe in a few months."

"Give it some more thought and let's decide later. I think it'll be good for both of us."

After promising to not shoot the idea down completely, Naomi kissed his cheek. With plans set to meet at his apartment later that evening for dinner, she raced off to her next appointment.

Naomi hated for any of her friends or family to see her in a bad mood. But she was emotionally numb, finding the loss of her crop and damage to her fields devastating. Fruit trees that had been blossoming on that land for years were gone. Sustainable land that had been nutrient rich was now lacking and the soil's water repellency had completely changed. She was grateful that no one had been harmed and the house was still standing. But having to rearrange payment to her investors, figure out where payroll would come from and work to move forward was proving to be more than she wanted to handle.

Later that night, when she finally made it to bed, she welcomed Patrick's presence, feeling immensely blessed to have him to lean on. He made love to her slowly, his body moving against hers like a well-tuned instrument. His touch was healing, his words in her ear loving and his embrace protective. She knew beyond any doubt that Patrick loved her as much as she loved him. They were good together and good for each other. And because they were so good together she knew when something wasn't quite right. Her very best friend was off his regular game.

After making love, they lay sprawled against each other, their limbs entangled. Sleep was elusive, both of them consumed with thought. She asked again what might be bothering him.

"I'm worried about you," he answered.

Naomi rolled over, throwing her bare leg atop his. "There's something else. Something you're not telling me. I can feel it."

Silence billowed between them, Patrick not bothering to respond.

"I have to ask you something," Naomi suddenly said, then paused.

"You can ask me anything. You know that."

"Do you think Garrison or Gisele could have had anything to do with the fire? Or maybe even Nolan?"

"Why would you ask me that?" He shifted upright, leaning on his elbow as he stared down at her.

"So, you've thought it possible, too?"

There was a moment of hesitation as Patrick pondered her comment. He had wondered if his old friends were capable of stooping so low. And suspecting that either could have done such a thing weighed heavily on his heart. He just didn't have the energy to say so to Naomi.

"Let the police continue their investigation. Let's not jump to any assumptions. We need to keep our focus on rebuilding."

"Why do I feel like there's something you're not telling me, Patrick?" Naomi asked.

There was another long pause, the mood between them becoming tense. Patrick took a deep inhalation and held it. When he finally let it go, Naomi was still studying him keenly.

"Garrison called me. It was Garrison being Garrison. He asked me about the fire and mentioned his father had told him that gasoline was involved. So yes, I have wondered. It just kills me that I would even have to question any of them."

"But you think he may have been responsible?"

"That's not what I said, Naomi. I said I've wondered. That's all."

She was still staring at him, the look she gave him suddenly feeling like a wall building between them. He was anxious to change the subject. "Baby, I know Garrison is capable of many things but in all honesty, I don't see him doing this. Garrison has always been more hot air than anything else, and Giselle, well, she's like a sheep. She just follows the crowd."

"But Nolan has no filters. And you've said he can be ruthless. So, he is quite capable, right?"

"I don't know, Naomi. I really don't think so."

"I get it. They were your family. Your friends. You miss them. It's perfectly understandable."

"It's more than that, baby. I've worked side by side with Nolan. I have always respected his integrity. He's not the sensitive type, but I've always found him to be aboveboard in business. Ruthless, in that he doesn't play games and will go after what he wants, but still aboveboard. I would hate to think that he could stoop that low."

"I get it. I do." She reached up to kiss Patrick's lips, ending the conversation.

Naomi fell into her own thoughts and rolled away from him, turning her back. Patrick eased against her, spooning himself snugly against her. Neither said anything else.

Jimmy Kimmel was in the middle of his monologue, the late-night talk show playing on the television in the corner of the room. An infomercial for men's hair plugs eventually lulled them both to sleep. When Patrick woke the next morning, Naomi was gone and a note was left on her pillow.

He jumped from the bed, and grabbed a quick shower and a fresh change of clothes. Reading the quickly scribbled lines a second time, he searched for his keys and then raced out the door. He would call her brother on his way across town, hoping that Noah would be able to join him.

Patrick instinctively knew that the day had already gone straight to hell and there was nothing he would could do to change that. Naomi was intent on justice and there would be no stopping her.

Chapter 14

Standing in the lobby of the Perry Group's executive offices, Naomi was second-guessing her decision to be there. It had all made perfect sense an hour earlier, but now she wasn't quite sure what she planned to do.

The glass-and-steel facility was one of the city's pride and joys. It was a stunning twenty-six-story office tower with a rooftop heliport and observation deck. The building's facade was covered in white granite and the interior boasted English all-wool carpets and exquisite Venetian chandeliers. It housed the family business and the church that Nolan had pastored since forever, plus a residential tower and a series of small businesses on the lower level.

Naomi could feel the security guard eyeing her, and she prayed that it was her good looks drawing his attention and not that she'd been fidgeting like a fish out of water since she'd arrived. She moved past the uniformed man toward the high-end jewelry store and pretended to window-shop.

Confronting Nolan Perry and his demon spawn had seemed completely logical when the idea came to her. She'd been deliberating over it since her conversation with Patrick the previous night. If any of the Perrys had been responsible for the fire on her property, she wanted to know. She needed to lay blame where it was due, and if that meant finding the answers on her own she was willing to do that. Now she was thinking that running up on her sperm donor and his other offspring might not be the way to go. She tossed a look over her shoulder, eyeing the security guy as he chatted up a tall blonde in skinny jeans and a white peasant blouse.

Naomi reached for the cell phone in her purse. There was a lengthy list of missed calls. Most were from Patrick and a few from her brother. She ignored them as she pushed the speed dial button for Natalie instead. Natalie would be less inclined to talk her out of doing something foolish. Natalie would fuel her desire to at least do something.

She stood with the cell phone pressed to her ear, staring into the jewelry store window as the phone rang on the other end.

Natalie answered on the fourth ring. "You are up bright and early, big sister. What's wrong?"

With her emotions already running high, Naomi bit down on her bottom lip, fighting not to cry. Hearing her sister's voice suddenly had her on emotional overload.

"Naomi? You're scaring me. Are you okay?"

"I think our father burned my property." Her voice was a hushed whisper as she shot a quick glance left and then right, to insure no one was eavesdropping on her conversation.

There was a swift inhalation of air on the other end. Naomi could hear the questions her sister was thinking but hadn't yet spoken aloud. She answered them before Natalie had a chance to ask. "I don't have any proof, but I can feel it in my gut. I know I'm right. I'm here at his office now and I was planning to confront him, but I'm getting cold feet. What if I'm wrong? What if I just want him to be guilty because I'm angry with him for deserting us?"

"Have you talked to Noah?"

"No."

"What does Patrick think?"

"Patrick, well, he…" Naomi paused, suddenly thinking about Patrick. She knew he was feeling conflicted, and after the sacrifice he'd already made on her behalf, she hated that he was still caught in the middle of drama that had nothing to do with him. He'd been forced to make a choice and he had chosen her. She couldn't ask for any more.

"You really need to talk this over with Patrick, Naomi."

"It's not that cut-and-dried, Natalie. He has a relationship with the Perry family. It was good between them until I came along."

"It wasn't that good or he would still be friends with

them. He loves you far more than he ever loved them and he's been proving it every day since you two met."

"So, what should I do? Should I go on up and confront Nolan?"

"Do you really think he's going to be honest with you, Naomi? I mean, think about it. He's been lying about us, and to us, our entire lives. Why would he start being truthful now just because you want him to be? You saw how that turned out for Norris Jean. She died still waiting for him to be truthful about something."

"You're right. I should go home."

"At least wait until Noah or Patrick can be there with you. You don't need to go through this alone, Naomi. Not when you have so much love wanting to be there for you."

Movement out of the corner of her eye drew Naomi's attention. She turned just in time to see Nolan Perry and his wife standing in front of the bank of elevators. The woman was chattering away about something as her husband stood focused on his iPhone.

Naomi turned abruptly as Nolan suddenly lifted his gaze, staring toward her. With her back to him she eased down the corridor to the gift shop, stepping through the entrance and out of sight.

"Naomi? You still there?"

"Yeah, I'm here," she said, refocusing on her conversation.

"Well, call me tomorrow. Tinjin and I are going back home to Paris in the morning so we'll be able to talk more tomorrow night. Okay?"

"Thanks, Natalie."

"Hey, we can always depend on each other. Isn't that what you used to tell me?"

Naomi chuckled softly. "I love you."

"I love you, too."

Disconnecting the call, Naomi turned to exit the small shop. Peeking first to see if the Perry family was still standing there, she was surprised to find Patrick sauntering in her direction. Her eyes widened as he moved swiftly to her side, reaching to wrap his arms around her.

"Good morning," he said, as he brushed a kiss against her cheek.

"What are you doing here?"

"I missed my woman this morning. I woke up in an empty bed and you weren't there."

"I left you a note. I told you where I would be."

"You did."

"So, you came to try and stop me."

Patrick shook his head. "Not at all. I came to be with you. Noah's on his way, too."

"You called my brother?"

"Someone once told me you Stallions are a formidable family because you always stick together."

Naomi smiled as he continued.

"Which is why I don't understand why you would think you needed to do this without them? And without me? Because, like it or not, I'm your family, too, Naomi."

She met the look he was giving her, his stern expression scolding, and shrugged. "Well, it doesn't matter. I was just about to head home. I shouldn't have come. I don't know what I was thinking."

Patrick lifted her chin and kissed her mouth. "That's not true. You wanted answers and we're going to get them for you. And we're going to get them today."

He clasped her hand, lacing their fingers together, then gestured with his head toward the elevators. Naomi hesitated, taking in deep breaths, air needed to fortify the strength she knew she required to confront her father. Then she squeezed Patrick's fingers.

Smiling down at her, he kissed her again, then turned. As they moved through the lobby, Noah suddenly burst through the glass entry doors. There was a moment's pause, a silent communication, and then he nodded his head.

"So, we're really doing this?" Noah asked, looking from one to the other.

Patrick shifted a questioning glance in her direction.

Naomi nodded back. "Yeah, we're really doing this."

Nolan's secretary greeted Patrick warmly, a bright smile creasing her face. The woman was stunning, tall and model thin, with skin the color of licorice.

"Mr. O'Brien, it's so good to see you again. You've been missed."

"It's good to see you, too, Brenda. Is he in his office?"

She nodded. "Is he expecting you? I don't see you on his calendar." Her eyes scanned her computer.

Patrick shook his head. "No, he's not expecting us."

The secretary reached for her phone as Patrick sauntered past her, pulling Naomi along with him.

"It's fine, Brenda. He'll see us," he said, tossing her a look over his shoulder.

"Mr. O'Brien, you can't… Mr. O'Brien!"

Noah winked at the woman as he followed behind them.

When the office door swung open unexpectedly, Nolan and his wife looked up from a stack of papers they were reviewing. As Patrick and Naomi pushed their way inside, the Perrys stole quick glances at each other, shock registering on their faces.

Patrick greeted them both politely. "Mr. Perry, Mrs. Perry, good morning. Excuse us for the interruption."

Brenda pushed through the door behind them. "I'm so sorry, Mr. Perry. Should I call security?"

Nolan held up a hand. "Have you lost your mind, son? What's the meaning of this?" He appeared confused as he recognized Naomi and her brother.

Patrick gestured for the secretary's attention. "Would you ask Garrison to join us, please, Brenda? And if the girls are in the building they should be invited, as well. Thank you."

Nolan waved the woman away. "I'm not sure what you're hoping to accomplish, Patrick, but this is not the time or the place."

Grace Perry interjected, "Perhaps you can come to the house later this week, Patrick?"

Naomi took a step forward. "This has nothing to do with Patrick, Mrs. Perry. This is about me and my—"

Grace interrupted, her curt tone bristling with indignation, "Young lady, I was not speaking to you! In fact, I'm not sure why you're even here."

Noah stepped up behind his sister. He pressed his hands against her shoulders, stalling the ire he knew was rising. "Excuse me, ma'am. I don't know you, but my sister hasn't spoken to you out of turn, so you need to show her the same respect."

Grace bristled. "Who are you?"

Naomi felt her brother tense. He took a breath and then answered, "My name is Noah Stallion and I'm your husband's eldest son."

Grace suddenly looked ill, the color having drained from her face. She shot her husband a look. Before she could respond Garrison came through the door, his sisters following on his heels.

"Hey, family, what's going on?" Garrison exclaimed. He hurried to Patrick's side, the two men slapping palms and bumping shoulders. "So, you've finally come to your senses?"

Patrick shook his head. "Why don't we all take a seat?"

"Well, hello there," Giselle exclaimed, as she brushed past Noah. She extended her hand. "I'm Giselle Perry. And who might you be?"

Naomi rolled her eyes. "Down, girl. You are definitely not his type!"

Giselle shot her a look. "What are you doing here? What's going on?"

Naomi shifted her gaze to Nolan. "Do you want to tell them or would you like for me to?"

"What I want, young lady, is for you three to get out of my office before I have you arrested for trespassing."

"Well, that's not going to happen, either," Patrick interjected.

An awkward silence suddenly blanketed the space. They each looked from one to the other, waiting to see who would jump first. Naomi finally broke the quiet. She moved to where Nolan stood, her arms crossed over her chest. "Why did you burn down my property? Why would you set fire to Norris Farms?"

"What is she talking about?" Georgina asked.

"Hey, don't talk crazy to my father. Patrick, you need to check your girl!" Garrison interjected.

Nolan held up his hand, his voice rising. "Everyone, quiet!" He met the stare Naomi was giving him. "Clearly, young lady, you've been misinformed. I'm not sure what you think you know but—"

Naomi interrupted him. "Why have you gone out of your way to hurt us? We were your family, too, and we didn't do anything to deserve what you did to us. We don't deserve what you're doing now."

"Family? What is she talking about?" Garrison shot Patrick a confused glance.

Nolan swiped his hand over his face. He'd gone bright red and looked like he might have a heart attack. He moved as if to make a run for the door. "I'm done here."

No one was prepared for the vase that flew past the man's head, just missing him. It hit the wall and shattered, the clinking of broken glass silencing the room.

"Baby, you okay?" Patrick said to Naomi between clenched teeth.

She cut him a glance, rage seeping from her eyes.

"He is not going to turn his back on us and disappear again. Not this time."

Noah chuckled nervously. "Just don't throw things, Naomi!"

Grace looked deflated as she rose from her seat and went to stand between Naomi and her husband. "That will be enough of that. Nolan, sit down."

"Don't tell me—"

The woman shouted, "Sit down now, Nolan!"

He bristled, but moved behind his desk and dropped into his leather executive chair.

Grace pointed toward the couch. "Garrison, you and your sisters sit over there. Naomi, if you and your brother would take those two leather chairs, please."

Looks darted back and forth as everyone waited for someone else to move first. Patrick finally stepped to Naomi's side as Grace leaned against her husband's oversize oak desk. The woman waited for her children to obey, and when everyone was seated, she continued, "We should have done this years ago, Nolan. Now, your daughter asked you a question and you need to answer her."

Nolan grunted. He shifted forward in his seat and back again, clearly uncomfortable. Everyone was staring at him and he was suddenly struggling for words.

Naomi repeated herself, "Were you responsible for the fire that destroyed my land?"

"No, I would not have done that," he answered.

"Did any of your children?"

"I know she's not talking about me," Giselle quipped.

Nolan shot the young woman an admonishing look.

He shook his head. "No, I can say beyond any reasonable doubt that none of my children were responsible."

Naomi shot Garrison a look. For the first time, there was something that seemed genuine in the look he gave her back.

He held his hands up as if surrendering and shook his head. "I didn't do it, Naomi. I swear. I'm a lot of things but I'm not an arsonist. Besides, Patrick's my brother, even if we do see things differently. I've got mad love for him, I just couldn't bring myself to be that low."

Giselle sighed. "We were joking when we said we should take her business out. We didn't really try to do it. At least I didn't."

Georgina shrugged. "I am so confused! I don't have a clue what any of you are talking about."

Naomi turned her attention back to Nolan. "Thank you."

Grace looked at her husband. "Now you need to answer her second question."

Nolan leaned forward, resting his elbows on the desktop. He dropped his head between his palms, covering his face. When he looked back up a tear had rolled down his cheek. Rising from his seat, he rounded the desk and went to stand before Naomi and Noah. He leaned back against the desk, his eyes shifting between them.

"I never meant to hurt any of you and I never meant to hurt your mother. You have to understand, it was a different time, and I didn't always make the right decisions."

He shifted his gaze toward the three on the sofa.

"Naomi and Noah are your half siblings. And there are three more. The twins, Nathaniel and Nicholas, and my baby girl, Natalie."

"Half siblings?" Garrison looked confused.

"Their mother and I were lovers. For many years. Norris Jean and I had five children together."

"Why didn't we ever know this?" Georgina questioned, her incredulous gaze sweeping around the room.

"Because your father refused to have anything to do with us. He abandoned us and our mother years ago," Noah said.

"I never abandoned you," Nolan declared.

"You never took care of us. You never supported us. What would you call that?"

The man looked confused. "I did support you. Your mother received money from me every month, right up until the day she died."

"Our mother never received a dime from you!" Naomi snapped. "How dare you tell that lie!"

"We struggled for years. While you and your other family were living well on your side of the tracks, we had nothing in the trailer park we grew up in. Nothing!" Noah added.

Nolan shook his head. "I don't know what your mother did with the money, but we paid her. We paid her very well. We made sure she…" He suddenly paused, turning to stare at his wife.

Grace sat with her eyes closed, tears streaming down her face. When she opened them, everyone in the room was staring at her.

"What did you do?" Nolan asked in a low voice.

Grace shook her head. "I had to protect my children first."

"First? Woman, what are you talking about?"

"I had to ensure their futures, and back then I didn't know what was going to happen."

"What are you saying?"

Her voice rose. "I'm saying everything wasn't always about that Stallion woman or your bastard children. That's what I'm saying."

A collective gasp echoed around the room. Naomi balled up her fists, looking like she was about to throw a punch. But Nolan looked like he was going to throw more than a fist.

He took a step toward his wife. "You never paid her, did you? You never sent Norris that money."

Grace hesitated, her chin lifting slightly in defiance. "No. I didn't."

Noah and Naomi exchanged a look. Their gazes shifted back to Nolan, who was visibly shaking.

Grace moved to the window, her arms wrapped protectively around her torso. "I need to start at the beginning so you'll all understand. Norris Jean and I were friends. Very good friends. My grandparents owned a laundry in Texas and Norris's mother, your grandmother, was a washwoman who worked for them. She used to bring Norris to work with her and we would play together. We had some of the best times!

"We tried to keep in contact when my family moved from Texas here to Utah, but it was a different era back then. We were pen pals for a while, but that didn't last long. I met Nolan shortly after we moved. I was very young, but even then I knew he and I were destined to be together."

She gave them all a weak smile as she continued, "His ministry was just starting out, but I could see the potential in him. He was destined to do great things. He came from a very prominent family and he was a great catch for any girl. I was smitten from the first moment I saw him.

"One summer the church sent him to Dallas to do ministry, and I gave him Norris Jean's information and asked him to contact her for me. And he did."

Nolan took up the story as he dropped into reflection. "Your mother was so beautiful! Everything about her was breathtaking. It was love at first sight for both of us. Her father had forbidden her to see me and well... we didn't listen. All we wanted was to be together. We didn't see any of the things that were supposed to keep us apart. It wasn't about race or money or anything else with us. We just loved each other. She became pregnant with you that summer, Noah, and we were so happy!"

Grace sniffed and then continued, "I was devastated when I found out. And angry. Angry at Norris Jean. Nolan and I were engaged to be married. She had no respect for our relationship. I convinced Nolan not to tell his parents, and I convinced Norris Jean that she shouldn't do anything to ruin his future. Him impregnating a black woman would have destroyed everything he had been working for. We couldn't let that happen."

Nolan shook his head. "When I came back to Utah, I brought your mother with me," he told Naomi and Noah. "We had a plan. We were going to marry, and if need be, we would have moved somewhere else. But then, out of nowhere, she refused. She threatened to take the baby and go back to Texas. I didn't know that Grace had gotten into her ear. Norris Jean just said that she wanted what was best for me. And apparently, what was best for me was what everyone else wanted. Before I knew it I was married to Grace. So Norris and I tried to make it work the only way we thought we could. We couldn't be together, but we couldn't stay away from each other."

"You wouldn't have had any of this if you hadn't married me," Grace snapped, waving her hands in the air. "Your father would have disowned you for even thinking about marrying her."

"You don't know what the hell I would have had," Nolan snapped.

"So, you knew about our mother the entire time?" Naomi met the woman's gaze. "And you stayed with him?"

"I loved Nolan. I stayed because...well..."

"Because you didn't want Norris to have what you had—the power, the prestige, the wealth..."

"I wanted your heart. I didn't have that. Norris had your love. You gave me the leftovers and I wouldn't have had that if I hadn't taken it." The bitter undertones of the woman's words didn't go unnoticed, Naomi bristling with ire.

"So, you stole the money our father meant for us to have?" Naomi asked.

Grace blew out a heavy sigh. "I thought if things got hard enough for her, Norris Jean would go back to Texas. To her family. But she didn't. She stayed. And in the back of my mind I knew there was always the chance that Nolan would choose her. And all of you. I needed to ensure that if that happened I'd be able to take care of my family."

Nolan flinched. "You selfish…" He caught himself, squelching the profanity that clearly threatened to spew out.

"No, selfish was always promising her that you would find a way for the two of you to be together. Selfish was thinking you could keep me in limbo while you tried to make things work with her. Selfish was you never trying to make *our* relationship work!"

Naomi cut her eyes from Grace to Nolan. "Mr. Perry, why did you stop coming to see her? Us? After Natalie was born we never saw you again. At least before that you would bring things, and Norris Jean was happy."

Nolan looked toward Naomi. "I don't know," he said, shrugging his shoulders. "I guess, if I'm honest, I'll admit I was a coward. Grace believed if the church found out, it would ruin my standing. This business was just beginning to take off and do well. It became a regular argument and I…well, I just gave up. I hated myself for it, but it wasn't fair of me to keep stringing your mother along. I thought maybe she'd find someone else and she could be happy. So, when Grace made me promise not to have anything else to do with Norris and all of you, I agreed. I thought it would be enough as long as I could support all of you, and Grace promised she would handle that. She swore she was sending your mother money every month to take care of you. And I trusted her."

He paused. "I trusted you." The couple locked gazes.

Grace shook her head. "Do you know what it's like to love a man who is in love with someone else? After everything I did for you? For us? And it was Norris Jean who was always in your head. You were always thinking about her. Wanting her. Wishing things were different. Someone needed to protect our name. To preserve your legacy. I did what I had to do."

Nolan shook his head. He moved to Naomi as she stood up from her seat. He cupped her face in his palms and trailed the pad of his thumb across her cheek. "I'm sorry," he said, his voice low. "I failed you. And I failed your mother. And I'm so very sorry."

Naomi's tears rained down, a sudden storm she hadn't expected. She felt Patrick wrap his arm around her waist as Nolan pressed a kiss to her forehead and then stepped away from her.

She and Patrick moved toward the door, Noah leading the way. She suddenly stopped, turning her attention back to the Perry family. The lot of them looked broken, weathered from the wind that had snapped them like twigs. Grace Perry was still standing at the window, staring out over the landscape. Naomi called her name.

"Mrs. Perry?"

"Yes?"

"Why did you burn down my farm?"

The woman bristled visibly. Her eyes skated around the room before settling back on Naomi's face. "When your father saw you at the auction, you were all he could talk about. How proud he was. How successful you had all become. How much you looked like your mother. I just wanted you gone."

"Grace!"

"Mom, how could you?"

Naomi nodded, turned and exited the room with Patrick and Noah close behind.

No one said anything as the trio rode the elevator down to the lobby. Outside, Patrick clutched her shoulders, looking her in the eye. "Baby, are you okay?"

She smiled. "I'm good."

"How did you know it was her?" Noah asked. "That she was the one responsible for the fire?"

Naomi shrugged. "I didn't. I took a guess. She just confirmed it."

Chapter 15

Since their encounter with Nolan Perry and his family, Naomi hadn't had anything to say about everything she'd learned. Despite Patrick's best efforts and those of Noah and her other siblings, she refused to talk about her father, the fire, Mrs. Perry or any of it. Instead, she'd thrown herself back into her work, every conversation starting and ending with horticulture and how that applied to her business model. She tested new raw organic recipes, kept the refrigerator stocked with fresh juices and smoothies and acted as if nothing had changed. She'd even begun a new video blog about organic eating that had attracted a very loyal following, taking the metaphor "busy as a bee" to new heights.

Patrick was still flying back and forth to Arizona with her and he enjoyed the life they were building together. After a very lengthy debate about him investing in the Utah farm, she'd taken him on as a partner, allowing him to give her an influx of cash to help with repaying her investors and restoring the soil and replanting the crop. Opening the co-op had been delayed, but they were still on track to make it happen.

When he came through the door of his apartment, Naomi was already there. He heard her in the bedroom, on the telephone. She was laughing, and he realized that despite his best efforts, she hadn't laughed that freely since before the fire. He was grateful to whomever it was that had her giggling so easily.

Since Naomi had taken up space in his apartment, every room felt different. The place was energized and alive, feeling more like a home. The many shades of gray were now peppered with vibrant reds and yellows and greens. She'd tossed pillows, draped tapestries, set out candles and filled the space with plants. There was artwork on the walls, pictures of his family and hers on the desktops. His cabinets were devoid of junk food, the fridge stocked with GMO-free fruits and vegetables, and even his beloved coffee was now organic. One month had made a major difference in his life and hers. Every change she'd introduced him to had been for the better, and now he was ready to make things between them permanent.

He grabbed a bottle of spring water from the refrigerator and moved toward the bedroom. Naomi was reclined against the pillows, her cell phone propped between her ear and shoulder. He blew her a kiss and waved, then turned to go back to the living room to give her some privacy. Waving back, she tapped the bed and gestured for him to join her. After crawling up on the mattress, he kissed her cheek, then fell back with his head in her lap.

Naomi was laughing again. "I can't wait to see those pictures. I can't imagine what that was like."

There was a pause as she listened to whoever was on the other end. Meanwhile she trailed her hand over his chest and under his shirt, lightly stroking the muscles of his six-pack. He twitched, her touch tickling him. She smiled down at him, winking, as his own grin widened.

"I will…Yes, ma'am…We're looking forward to it. Do you want to speak with him? He just walked through the door."

Patrick tossed her a look, a question forming as he tried to figure out who she was talking to.

"I'll let him know. I promise. You have a good night."

Disconnecting the call, Naomi tossed her phone to the other side of the bed. "Hey, honey! How was your day?"

He laughed. "Didn't we work together all day?"

"We did. But I don't know how things went after I left and you went to gym."

"The gym was good. I had fun with the equipment and I even ran into Garrison."

"Oh. How is he?"

"Garrison. He'll never change."

Naomi chuckled softly. "Well, let's hope you two can rebuild your friendship so you can be a good influence on him."

"Have you thought about trying to build a relationship with your other family? Maybe talk to Nolan or Garrison and the girls?"

Naomi's smile disappeared. She didn't bother to answer the question, changing the subject instead. "Aren't you going to ask me what I did this evening?"

Hating that he'd put a frown on her face after she'd seemed so happy, Patrick didn't press the issue. "So, how was your day, babe?"

"My day was exceptionally productive. I didn't go to the gym! What I did do was plan a vacation for us." Her frown shifted, the light returning to her eyes. "A much-needed vacation!"

Patrick sat upright. "A vacation?"

"Well, more of an extended getaway. A long weekend of sorts. We're flying out tomorrow. Then we'll go back to Phoenix on Monday."

"Where are we going?"

"Miami!"

Patrick twisted to face her. "Miami? Really?"

"Yes. And your mother said to make sure you check your emails. She's sending you a list of things she wants you to bring her."

"You talked to my mother?"

"I did indeed. That was her on the phone. She said to tell you she loves you and she can't wait to see you."

"You spoke to my mother!"

"I can't wait to meet her," Naomi said, as she leaned to give him a kiss.

Wrapping his arms around her, he rolled until he'd pulled her down against him, his mouth still dancing with hers. She tasted sweet, like milk chocolate and berries. His eyes widened as he pulled back from her.

"You made dessert!"

Naomi laughed. "Really, Patrick O'Brien. You kiss me and all you can think of is dessert?"

He drew his hand through her hair, pulling her back to him. He licked her lips, then gently suckled on her bottom lip and then her top. His touch became heated and intoxicating as their tongues tangled inside her mouth and then his. When he finally pulled back, Naomi was gasping for air. "Parfait!" he exclaimed, lifting his eyebrows in jest. "You made fruit parfaits with cacao bits."

The joy in Naomi's eyes as she laughed heartily made his heart sing. "I left you one in the refrigerator," she said. "I'm actually surprised you missed it!"

That night, dessert lasted long past the parfait. Naomi was his chocolate delight and then some. They made the sweetest love, over and over again, until exhaustion swept in, sending them both into a deep sleep. When the sun rose, the two were still curled tightly around each other, limbs so tightly entangled that it was hard to tell where one began and the other ended. They had danced merrily together in each other's dreams, and as Naomi shifted her body even closer to his, Patrick couldn't imagine himself not waking with her by his side.

Chapter 16

Naomi was still laughing as Patrick ran last-minute errands, trying to find the items his mother had insisted he bring home with him. Most were tourist trinkets: key chains with the Salt Lake City logo, a man's size large Utah Jazz T-shirt, Cox brand whipped honey flavored with raspberry. And collegiate ice cream, the Aggie Blue Mint, a blue ice cream with pieces of Oreo cookie and white chocolate mixed in.

Patrick tossed up his hands. "How are we supposed to bring ice cream? This is ridiculous."

"I have a great insulated cooler and all we'll need to do is pack a ton of ice around it. It will be fine!"

"Why do I feel like you two are up to something?"

"Who?"

"You and my mother!"

"Because we are," Naomi said with a little giggle. She brushed her body against his and wrapped her arms around his waist. She reached to kiss his lips. "Your mother and I are going to have so much fun giving you a hard time!"

Patrick shook his head. Before he could respond, the moment was interrupted by the doorbell sounding. They exchanged a questioning look.

"Are you expecting someone?" Patrick asked.

Naomi shook her head. "No. You?"

He released the hold he had on her and moved to the door. He peered through the peephole, then stepped back, clearly surprised. Naomi came close, eyeing him curiously.

She mouthed, "Who is it?"

Patrick smiled as he pulled the door open. Garrison and his sister Georgina stood on the other side.

"Hey," Garrison said, giving him a slight wave. "Is this a bad time?"

Patrick shook his head. "Actually, it's not the best. We were just about to head out. Naomi and I are going out of town for the weekend."

"We were hoping to talk to Naomi."

Naomi moved to Patrick's side. "Please, come in," she said, looking from one to the other. She took a step back as they complied. "What brings you by?"

Georgina stepped past her brother. "Hi," she said, her voice cracking with nervous energy. "We won't take up much of your time, I promise."

"It's not a problem," Naomi said with a smile. "Come, have a seat."

The young woman shook her head. "We're not going to stay." She and Garrison exchanged a quick look.

Garrison nodded. "Look, I'm not really good at stuff like this, so if I screw it up I hope you'll forgive me. We just wanted to say how sorry we are for everything that has happened. Our parents being buttheads and all."

Georgina rolled her eyes. "You can always count on Garrison to screw things up."

Patrick laughed. "He does have a way with words."

Naomi smiled again.

"What Garrison is trying to say is that we hope you and Noah and the others will give us a chance. We'd like to get to know you and for you to get to know us."

"The good stuff about us. Not the screwed-up stuff," Garrison interjected. "I'm sure my buddy here has already filled you in on that."

They all laughed easily.

"You might not have heard, but our mother was arrested and charged with setting that fire to your property."

Naomi's expression fell, the light dimming ever so slightly in her eyes. "I did hear. I'm very sorry."

"Don't be. Father turned her in," Georgina said matter-of-factly. "He also filed for divorce."

Garrison nodded. "He's really not a bad guy," he said softly. "They were always so cold to each other that we used to make jokes about why they married each other. Now we know…"

"Where's Giselle?" Patrick queried.

"Doing that diva thing she does. She's not there yet. You know she already had issue with the inheritance being split three ways. Discovering that she's now only getting one-eighth has completely devastated her." Garrison chuckled.

Patrick laughed.

"Well," Naomi said, "I appreciate you coming by. I really do."

Georgina nodded. "We know it's going to take some time, but we really want us all to be a family. At least, maybe try? I need a big brother who isn't dopey all the time and Noah seemed like a really great guy."

"Who are you calling dopey?"

The two women exchanged a hug.

Garrison and Georgina left as quickly as they'd come.

Patrick tossed Naomi a look. "You good?"

She grinned. "I'm great."

Patrick was a mama's boy and Naomi loved that about him. Zora O'Brien was everything he had described and then some. She had Naomi at her first hello. She was small in stature, but her magnetic presence was large and abundant, and her hundred-watt smile lit up the room.

They had been there for barely half a day when she'd insisted on washing and retwisting Naomi's dreadlocks. The products she used had been made in her kitchen, the conditioner a mix of avocado, coconut milk and olive oil. When she was done, Naomi's hair felt luxurious and the freshly twisted strands looked amazing.

It was their last afternoon there, the trip ending early the next morning. Naomi had danced hard, played hard and laughed until tears ran from her eyes. Patrick had taken great joy in showing off the Little Havana neighborhood he'd been raised in. She'd fallen in love with the Agustin Gainza Arts and Studio, purchasing several prints from the artist's Mulata series. She'd watched skilled Cuban cigar rollers at El Credito Cigar Factory and had eaten more than her fair share of plantains and homemade *mamey*-fruit-and-flan ice cream, and continued to drink *guarapo* juice like water. She'd even strayed from her diet to taste the guava *pastelito* Patrick's mother was renowned for. It was one of the best weekends she'd ever had. The time spent with Patrick's family was reminiscent of what she and her siblings had found with their Dallas cousins. It reminded her of just how important her family was to her.

Everything about the O'Brien home spoke to Naomi's esthetic. It was comfortable and casual, filled with light and color and the most amazing smells. And the music! The music was constant. Bass-heavy tunes that inspired dancing and movement and simply made her smile with glee. Family came and went without knocking and children played in every room. Naomi imagined that for any kid, growing up in such an environment had to feel like a nonstop party.

Across the room, Patrick was catching up with a cousin, the man jabbering away in English and Spanish. Patrick was trying to look attentive but losing that battle. Naomi laughed as he caught her eye, his smile canyon deep. He twisted a finger at the edge of his temple, amusement painting his expression. The other man laughed and slapped him on the back.

Seeing Patrick so relaxed and carefree was a sheer joy. He was comfortable and the environment suited him to a T. She had worried about him losing his job, and when he hadn't rushed to find another, seeming to give up his interest in returning to a courtroom, she'd felt immense guilt. They'd had many discussions, until she'd felt okay about what he said he wanted. He was officially on retainer for both farms and his legal skills had come in quite handy. He was also sexy as hell when he donned his boots and jeans to help her out in the fields.

After he'd gone with her to the Perry offices, it felt as if they'd hit a small speed bump. She blamed herself for that, not wanting to open up about the encounter with her father. She hadn't wanted to talk, and Patrick allowed her the time she needed to process it all. But in that moment, she knew they were right on track with each other, and she would not have had it any other way.

She skipped across the room and pulled him away. Together the two danced to the center of the room. They were wrapped warmly around each other and there was no denying the love they shared. Naomi pressed her mouth to his and kissed him eagerly. "I love you, Patrick O'Brien!"

He chuckled softly. "I love you more, Naomi Stallion."

"Your mother says you're going to ask me to marry you. I keep waiting for it but you seem to be taking forever, and you know I'm not a patient woman."

Patrick laughed. "She did, did she?"

"I did!" Zora laughed with them. She was leaning against the fireplace, watching them closely.

Patrick's father moved to his wife's side and wrapped his arms around her. He kissed her sweetly, then called across the room, "Patrick, you heard your mother!"

Patrick nodded. He lifted his hand and called out for everyone's attention. When the room quieted, with only the soft sound of the stereo playing in the background, Patrick reached into his pocket and pulled out a small velvet box. He suddenly dropped down onto one knee, taking Naomi's hand into his own.

Naomi's eyes widened and she felt the breath fly from her lungs. "Patrick! We were teasing!"

"I wasn't," he said softly. He kissed the back of her fingers. "Naomi Stallion, I love you. I love your quiet strength. And your exuberant spirit. I love how committed you are to others. I love everything about you. You have become my world and I can't imagine not having a future with you. Will you marry me, Naomi? Will you make me the happiest man in the whole wide world?"

"Yes, yes, yes, yes, yes!" Naomi cried. "Yes!" She jumped up and down, squealing with glee!

"Congratulations!" Zora called out to them both. And then she sang them the prettiest love song.

Epilogue

The wedding planner they'd hired had transformed Norris Farms into a magical wonderland. It was over-the-top and simply gorgeous. Going into the planning process, Naomi hadn't any idea what she'd wanted. But after listening to everything she and Patrick liked, their planner, Jacquie, had worked an absolute miracle.

Standing in the front window of the old homestead, watching the guests arrive, Naomi was in complete awe. It was a secret garden of vibrant color and she couldn't believe how beautiful it all was. When it was time, she would follow a path of flower petals from the front door of the homestead to the ceremony site, escorted by her brother Noah.

The ceremony would take place in front of the old barn. They would exchange their vows beneath an arch of natural vines, greenery, bright florals and lace ribbons that billowed in the breeze. After the "I dos," there would be old-fashioned pig pickin', without the pig, in the barn, with dancing and dining until sunset. Patrick's parents were in charge of the music and his mother had promised to perform.

Brightly colored paper lanterns hung from the barn's ceiling, complementing the fresh floral arrangements that adorned the tables. There was tons of crystal, fine china, cloth napkins, a five-tiered wedding cake and an extraordinary vegetarian menu. Naomi was bubbling with excitement, wanting it to be over so she could say she was Patrick O'Brien's wife.

"You need to get into your dress," Natalie said, interrupting her thoughts.

"Is it time?"

Her sister grinned. "That's why you need to get into your dress."

Naomi laughed. "So now we're being funny. You know I'm nervous, Natalie."

"You're going to be fine."

"It looks like everyone was able to make it. I was worried."

Natalie shook her head. "Come on," she said, as she pointed Naomi toward the back bedroom.

Adjusting the curtains, Naomi turned. As she did, the front door swung open and her brother Noah came through.

"Shouldn't you be dressed?" he asked, noting the white terry robe she wore.

"She just has to slip her gown on," Natalie said.

He nodded. "There's someone here who wants to see you."

Naomi eyed him curiously. "Who?"

Noah's gaze bounced from one woman to the other. "Nolan's here."

Naomi's eyes widened. "He came?"

Her brother nodded. "Everyone's here. So, can he come in?"

She looked toward Natalie and back to her brother, feeling anxiety waft over her. She suddenly wanted Patrick there so he could tell her what to do.

Natalie answered for her, "Let her put her gown on. Tell him to come in and she'll be back out in a minute."

Noah nodded. He moved to her side and kissed her forehead, hugging her tightly. "I'm so happy for you. Patrick is a great guy. You done good!"

Naomi laughed. "Thank you." She took a big breath and hurried after her sister.

Behind the closed door, she dropped down on the bed, clutching the spread with both hands. "I never thought I'd see this day."

"You mean your wedding?"

Naomi shook her head. "Our father being at my wedding."

Natalie smiled. "I like him. I know we still have a lot of years to make up for, but I like him. He's going to come to Paris next month to spend time with me and Tinjin."

"Looks like he's making the rounds. He was in Los Angeles last week with Nathaniel and Nicholas. I hear they had a really good time."

Natalie nodded. "Noah's talking to him more, too. It's just going to take some time."

"I can't get past the fact that he didn't try to have a relationship with us. No matter what the circumstances, he didn't try."

"No, he didn't. But he's trying now. Let that count for something. What was that our mother use to say? When you know better, you do better?"

"Norris Jean never said that."

Natalie laughed. "It sounded like something she would say." She reached for the garment bag that hung on the closet door. After sliding down the zipper, she pulled out the gown that her husband had designed especially for Naomi.

Tears instantly misted her sister's eyes. "Natalie, it's so beautiful!"

"And the shoes are to die for!" she exclaimed, pointing out the low-heeled pumps adorned with crystals and pearls.

Naomi laughed. "Yes, your husband is a shoe master!"

Minutes later Natalie stood staring at her reflection in the full-length mirror. The dress was everything a modern romantic with a wanderlust spirit could wish for. It was a simple sheath design of barley-colored lace over satin. The sleeves were ethereal, the neckline plunging, with a satin ribbon tied around the waist. It was pretty and she looked stunning in it.

"Your dreadlocks are incredible," Natalie said, as she adjusted the gold adornments crimped sporadically through the length.

"Patrick's mother has this line of natural hair products that's absolutely amazing. I keep telling her she needs to start selling it."

"I want to try some!"

"There's plenty in my bathroom. Just take them. Let me know what you think. I want to carry it at the farm, and Patrick has agreed to help her bring it to market."

There was a knock on the door. Noah's voice echoed on the other side. "You're going to be late!"

Natalie pulled it open. "She's fine. Stop making her nervous."

"I wasn't the one giving everyone a lecture last night about being on time."

Naomi turned, and Noah saw her for the first time. Whatever else he was about to say was suddenly caught in his throat. "Wow!" he said finally. "Wow!"

Both his sisters smiled.

"You are beautiful," Nolan Perry suddenly said, standing in the doorway. "Absolutely beautiful. Your mother would be so proud."

Tears sprang to Naomi's eyes. She fanned her hand in front of her face to stop them from falling and ruining her makeup. "Thank you."

"I didn't mean to interrupt, but I have something for you."

Noah stepped into the room, moving to take Natalie's hand. Their father followed, easing his way to Naomi's side.

He looked older than she remembered, Naomi thought as they stood eyeing each other. Older and less intimidating. There was something gentle about his eyes. Something she often saw in her brothers, when they were at their best. She couldn't help but wonder how it might have been different if he'd made different choices, had loved her mother more and had just been a better man.

He pulled a large velvet box from the inside pocket of his blazer. Inside rested a multistrand pearl necklace with a gold clasp and an integrated diamond dome bow pendant. Naomi gasped, unable to catch the tears that finally fell.

"I remember this," she said. "You gave it to our mother."

He nodded. "I did. They belonged to your great-grandmother. Norris Jean gave them back and told me to give them to her on our wedding day. She let you wear them for a minute in those pink bunny pajamas you loved so much. I remember you cried when she made you take them off."

Natalie rushed to pat the tears that mottled her sister's makeup as the older man continued, "I never got the chance to give them to your mother, but I thought she wouldn't mind if I gave them to you."

"Oh, she would have minded!" both women chimed in unison.

Laughter rang throughout the room.

Turning, Naomi bent slightly at the knees, lifting her locks just enough for her father to secure the pearls around her neck. She glanced at her sister and brother for approval. "How do they look?"

Noah grinned. "Perfect."

"Patrick is a fine young man," Nolan concluded. "But he's definitely getting the better end of the deal!"

Naomi smiled. "Thank you."

The man nodded. "I'll go find my seat," he said, as he turned and made his exit.

The wedding planner suddenly came through the door. "Showtime!" she exclaimed. She held two stunning floral bouquets, passing the larger one to Naomi and the other to Natalie.

Jacquie gave directions as music suddenly sounded through the air. "Natalie, you first, and then, Noah, you'll guide your sister down the aisle."

Noah nodded and extended his elbow. As Naomi clasped her fingers around his arm, he leaned in to whisper in her ear, "You know, usually a girl wants her father to do this."

Naomi snapped her head to stare at him. "Did he say something to you?"

Her brother shook his head. "I just didn't want you thinking you would hurt my feelings if that was what you wanted. Because you'll only get to do this one time." He smiled. "At least we hope that's the case," he muttered softly.

Naomi took in a deep breath and then a second. Her brother's timing always gave her reason to pause. Because as a little girl she had thought about a father walking her down the aisle. Back then she would have settled for any father, as long as he was willing to acknowledge her as his. As Nolan had made his exit, stepping down off the porch to go find his seat, the thought had crossed her mind again. She took another deep breath as her brother squeezed her hand.

Following the flower petals, Naomi felt herself begin to shake. Noah tightened the hold he had on her, his strength fueling her own.

As they rounded the corner toward the barn, the view took Naomi's breath away. Every seat was filled with their family and friends. Jacquie had decorated the white folding chairs with lace slipcovers and multicolored ribbons. It was just dressy enough and comfortably casual.

The music suddenly changed and the wedding march announced her arrival. The crowd came to their feet, everyone turning to gaze at her. Garrison stood at the front with Patrick, who was grinning from ear to ear. As Natalie finally made it to the makeshift altar, she turned to give Naomi an encouraging smile.

Every one of her Stallion cousins had made the trip to support her. Patrick's Cuban Cajun relatives were front and center, and Nolan stood with Giselle and Georgina.

From where she stood, Naomi locked eyes with Patrick. He looked like pecan ice cream and butterscotch, a delectable confection with a big bow and her name engraved on the name tag. He was dressed in the most perfect brown silk suit, with a white dress shirt opened at the neck. They'd opted for no tie, but a tan pocket hankie was folded in an intricate design. As they stood staring at each other, every ounce of her anxiety faded into oblivion.

"You good?" Noah asked, his voice low.

Naomi nodded. "Yes." She shifted her gaze to her brother. "So, you really don't mind if I replace you right now?"

Noah smiled. "Do what you have to do, little sister!"

She met his eyes, tears misting her own. She took a deep breath, fighting not to cry the ugly cry. "I want to get married to the most amazing man, and I think I need my father to walk me down the aisle."

Noah leaned to kiss her cheek, his lips lingering as he gave her a hug. With a nod, he stepped away, walked over to Nolan and spoke quietly. Surprise washed over the patriarch's face as he turned to stare at her. Naomi smiled, her head bobbing up and down.

Making his way to the aisle, Nolan moved to Naomi's side and extended his arm. "Thank you," he said as she took it.

She smiled again, muttering under her breath, "This doesn't mean we don't still have some things to work on."

Nolan nodded. "I understand."

"You aren't completely off the hook yet. At least not with me."

"Okay."

"And don't expect me to be calling you Dad when this is all over, because that probably won't happen."

"I understand."

She took another deep breath. "Thank you for doing this."

"I love you, Naomi."

At the end of the aisle, Nolan glided Naomi's hand into Patrick's. The two men exchanged a look.

"Be good to my daughter," Nolan said, then he winked and turned to go back to his seat.

Patrick nodded, his smile so bright it could have illuminated the darkest sky. "Yes, sir." He shifted his gaze back to Naomi, knowing in that moment he never again wanted to take his eyes off her. She was easily the most stunning woman he had ever known and she would forever be all his.

"I'm very proud of you," he said, tilting his head after Nolan.

Her head dipped slightly as she gave him a look.

He chuckled softly. "I love you, my sweet Stallion!"

"I love you more," Naomi said, as she wrapped her arms around his neck and lifted her face to kiss his lips.

The pastor leaned in, his voice loud. "I love you both. Now, let's save some of that for when I pronounce you husband and wife."

* * * * *

Check out the previous books in THE STALLIONS *series by Deborah Fletcher Mello:*

SEDUCED BY A STALLION
FOREVER A STALLION
MY STALLION HEART
STALLION MAGIC
A STALLION'S TOUCH

Available now from Harlequin Kimani Romance!

KIMANI™
ROMANCE

COMING NEXT MONTH
Available September 26, 2017

#541 NEVER CHRISTMAS WITHOUT YOU
by Nana Malone and Reese Ryan
This collection features two sizzling holiday stories from fan-favorite authors. Unwrap the ultimate gift of romance as two couples explore the magic of true love at Christmas.

#542 TEMPTED AT TWILIGHT
Tropical Destiny • by Jamie Pope
Nothing fires up trauma surgeon Elias Bradley like the risk of thrilling adventure. But when he meets Dr. Cricket Warren, she awakens emotions that take him by surprise. And now she's having his baby… He's ready to step up, but can they turn a fantasy into a lifetime of romance?

#543 THE HEAT BETWEEN US
Southern Loving • by Cheris Hodges
Appointed to head Atlanta's first-ever jazz festival, marketing guru Michael "MJ" Jane sets out to create an annual event to rival New Orleans. Even if that means hiring her crush and former marine Jamal Carver to run security. Can love keep Jamal and MJ in harmony…forever?

#544 SIZZLING DESIRE
Love on Fire • by Kayla Perrin
Lorraine Mitchell cannot forget her heated encounter with firefighter Hunter Holland. Weeks later, she is stunned to discover that his father—a former patient of hers—has left her a large bequest! Despite mutual mistrust, reviving their spark might ignite a love that's as deep as it is scorching…

Get 2 Free Books,
Plus 2 Free Gifts —
just for trying the
Reader Service!

YES! Please send me 2 FREE Harlequin® Kimani™ Romance novels and my 2 FREE gifts (gifts are worth about $10 retail). After receiving them, if I don't wish to receive any more books, I can return the shipping statement marked "cancel." If I don't cancel, I will receive 4 brand-new novels every month and be billed just $5.69 per book in the U.S. or $6.24 per book in Canada. That's a savings of at least 12% off the cover price. It's quite a bargain! Shipping and handling is just 50¢ per book in the U.S. and 75¢ per book in Canada.* I understand that accepting the 2 free books and gifts places me under no obligation to buy anything. I can always return a shipment and cancel at any time. The free books and gifts are mine to keep no matter what I decide.

168/368 XDN GLWV

Name _____ (PLEASE PRINT)

Address _____ Apt. #

City _____ State/Prov. _____ Zip/Postal Code

Signature (if under 18, a parent or guardian must sign)

Mail to the **Reader Service**:
IN U.S.A.: P.O. Box 1341, Buffalo, NY 14240-8531
IN CANADA: P.O. Box 603, Fort Erie, Ontario L2A 5X3

Want to try two free books from another line?
Call 1-800-873-8635 or visit www.ReaderService.com.

*Terms and prices subject to change without notice. Prices do not include applicable taxes. Sales tax applicable in NY. Canadian residents will be charged applicable taxes. Offer not valid in Quebec. This offer is limited to one order per household. Books received may not be as shown. Not valid for current subscribers to Harlequin® Kimani™ Romance books. All orders subject to approval. Credit or debit balances in a customer's account(s) may be offset by any other outstanding balance owed by or to the customer. Please allow 4 to 6 weeks for delivery. Offer available while quantities last.

Your Privacy—The Reader Service is committed to protecting your privacy. Our Privacy Policy is available online at www.ReaderService.com or upon request from the Reader Service.

We make a portion of our mailing list available to reputable third parties that offer products we believe may interest you. If you prefer that we not exchange your name with third parties, or if you wish to clarify or modify your communication preferences, please visit us at www.ReaderService.com/consumerschoice or write to us at Reader Service Preference Service, P.O. Box 9062, Buffalo, NY 14240-9062. Include your complete name and address.

KROM17R2

SPECIAL EXCERPT FROM

Flirting with a gorgeous stranger at the bar is how Lorraine Mitchell celebrates her longed-for newly single status. One-night stands usually run hot and wild before quickly flaming out, but Lorraine cannot forget her heated encounter with firefighter Hunter Holland. And reviving their spark just might ignite a love that's as deep and true as it is scorching...

Read on for a sneak peek at
SIZZLING DESIRE,
the next exciting installment in author
*Kayla Perrin's **LOVE ON FIRE** series!*

"You know why I'm here tonight," Lorraine said to Hunter as they neared the bar. "What brings you here?"

"I'm new in town," Hunter explained.

"Aah. Are you new to California?" Lorraine asked. "Did you move here from another state?"

"I did, yes. But I'm not new to Ocean City. I grew up here, then moved to Reno when I hit eighteen. I lived and worked there for sixteen years, and now I'm back. I'm a firefighter."

That explained why he was in such good shape. Firefighters were strong, their bodies immaculately honed in order to be able to rescue people from burning buildings and other disastrous situations. No wonder he had come to her aid in such a chivalrous way.

KPEXP0917

She swayed a little—deliberately—so she could wrap her fingers tighter around his arm. Yes, she was shamelessly copping a feel. She barely even recognized herself.

"Oops," Hunter said, securing his hand on her back to make sure she was steady. "You okay?"

"I'm fine," Lorraine said. "You're so sweet." *And so hot.* So hot that she wanted to smooth her hands over his muscular pecs for a few glorious minutes.

She turned away from him and continued toward the bar. What was going on with her? It must be the alcohol making her react so strongly to this man.

Though the truth was, she didn't care what was bringing out this reaction in her. Because every time Hunter looked at her, she felt incredibly desirable—something she hadn't felt with Paul since the early days of their marriage. But unlike her ex-husband, Hunter's attraction for her was obvious in that dark, intense gaze. Every time their eyes connected, the chemistry sizzled.

Lorraine's heart was pounding with excitement, and it was a wonderful feeling after all the pain and heartache she'd gone through recently. It was nice to feel the pitter-patter of her pulse because of a guy who rated eleven out of ten on the sexy scale.

Lorraine veered to the left to sidestep a group of women. And all of a sudden, her heel twisted beneath her body. This time, she started to go down in earnest. Hunter quickly swooped his arms around her, and the next thing she knew, he was scooping her into his arms.

"Oh, my God," she uttered. "You're not carrying me—"

Don't miss SIZZLING DESIRE
by Kayla Perrin, available October 2017
wherever Harlequin® Kimani Romance™
books and ebooks are sold!

LOVE
Harlequin
romance?

Join our Harlequin community to share your thoughts and connect with other romance readers!

Be the first to find out about promotions, news, and exclusive content!

Sign up for the Harlequin e-newsletter and download a free book from any series at

www.TryHarlequin.com

CONNECT WITH US AT:

Harlequin.com/Community

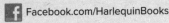 Facebook.com/HarlequinBooks

Twitter.com/HarlequinBooks

Instagram.com/HarlequinBooks

Pinterest.com/HarlequinBooks

ReaderService.com

 **HARLEQUIN**®

**ROMANCE WHEN
YOU NEED IT**

HSOCIAL2017

Want to give in to temptation with
steamy tales of irresistible desire?

Check out **Harlequin® Presents®,
Harlequin® Desire** and
Harlequin® Kimani™ Romance books!

New books available every month!

CONNECT WITH US AT:

Harlequin.com/Community

 Facebook.com/HarlequinBooks

 Twitter.com/HarlequinBooks

 Instagram.com/HarlequinBooks

 Pinterest.com/HarlequinBooks

ReaderService.com

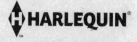

**ROMANCE WHEN
YOU NEED IT**

PGENRE2017